The Ruthless Groom

Monica Murphy

CHAPTER ONE

Charlotte

THE MOMENT I enter the suite, I'm turning the deadbolt on the door, my breathing harsh in the otherwise silent hotel room. I glance over at the bed, the messy sheets and rumpled pillows and memories of last night come at me, one after another.

Perry's mouth all over my body. Between my legs. The look on his face when he first entered me.

A shiver steals over me and I tell myself to focus.

After I wash my hands of the sticky coffee leftover from me tossing it at Seamus, I pace the hotel room, constantly checking my phone, tempted to call Perry and ask him if he's closer. The smug look on Seamus's face still haunts me and I open my browser on my phone, entering two words before I start searching.

Constantine Morelli.

A bunch of articles appear, mostly about various business deals. They've been archrivals for years from what I can tell, and the two families hate each other with a burning passion.

I knew this. From the very start I could tell there was tension between them whenever a Morelli showed up or was mentioned. Yet I also know there are various Morellis attending our wedding in a few short hours.

The Constantines are the type who keep their friends close and their enemies closer.

Are there McTiernans in attendance as well? It's a last name that's never been mentioned once since this entire situation started. I would've noticed. It's hard to forget the name of the man who took your virginity and lied to you the entire time you were together.

Anger suffusing me, I close out that tab and enter another two words into the browser, hitting search.

Seamus McTiernan.

I haven't done a Google search on him in months. First, because I banned myself after being in such a dark depression over our disaster of a relationship. Second, the last six weeks or so, I've been a little busy planning a wedding and getting to know my future husband.

As I scroll, I realize there still aren't many things written about Seamus. A couple of images of the Morelli and McTiernan clan gathered together, with him standing in the background, his face almost nondescript, the photo is so blurry. His name listed at the various institutions he's worked at in the past, though his image never accompanies those mentions. There are hardly any mentions of him at all.

His online presence is weak and that immediately makes me suspicious.

Is that on purpose? What is Seamus hiding? I wonder if he's still with his girlfriend. They'd been together a long time, I could tell. She treated him with a familiarity that comes with many years of being a couple.

Yet, in the coffee shop, he spoke of me as if he's always kept tabs on me.

That's…

Creepy.

There's a rapid-fire knock on the heavy door that startles me enough it makes me gasp. I run to the door, throwing it open at the same exact moment I remember Perry's warning that I should open it for no one else but him. And it's not Perry standing in front of me.

It's my mother.

"Darling!" She pushes past me and rushes inside the suite while I stand there gaping at her, sagging against the door. Incredibly grateful that it wasn't Seamus. She turns to face me, her gaze drifting over me, her expression dismayed. "Looks like you spilled something."

I glance down, noticing the light brown splattered pattern of coffee on my sweatshirt.

"You should've already showered by now, Charlotte. There's a lot of prep involved today," she continues.

"I just woke up," I lie as I slowly close the door, watching as she glances around the room, her nose faintly wrinkled.

"It's so dark in here." She marches over to the windows and yanks open the curtains, the bright sunny morning light making me wince. "There. That's much better."

"You're here early," I say weakly, wishing I had that coffee in hand after all. I'm going to need plenty of caffeine to get through this.

"I realized ten o'clock wasn't early enough to start this very important day. I called everyone last night and changed the time to nine," she explains.

"You didn't call me." I scroll through my past

notifications, realizing that oops, she did actually call. And I ignored it. Looks like she left a voicemail too.

Which I also ignored—probably because I was having sex with my almost-husband.

I can't help but smile. For once, I don't feel nervous or unsettled when I think about Perry. It actually seems...right that we're doing this. Getting married.

My stomach swarms with butterflies as the importance of today dawns on me. I'm getting married.

Married.

By tonight, I'll be known as Charlotte Constantine. This is a big deal.

Huge.

My smile fades. I hate that Seamus had to show up and taint the morning. I hate worse that Perry is speeding back toward the hotel, most likely worried sick about me.

Opening up my text messages, I send him a quick one.

Everything's okay. My mother is with me. I'll tell you what happened later.

There's another knock on the door and I rush to answer it, looking through the peephole this time around.

"It's the porter with my luggage," Mother announces just as I visually confirm that she's right. "The makeup artists and stylists are right behind me. They'll be here any minute. Caroline and Tinsley will be here soon too."

I open the door for the hotel employee who offers me a sheepish smile as he brings in the loaded bellman cart into the room. It's going to turn chaotic in here in a matter of minutes and I can definitely guarantee I won't get a chance to talk to Perry if he shows up—which he probably will. I won't be able to explain everything that happened and I hate that.

I hate it.

"Go take a shower," Mother demands once the porter leaves the room with his more than generous tip. "You need to get ready. But don't wash your hair! It'll be easier to work with if it's a little bit dirty."

"I washed it yesterday," I say, in a daze as I walk over to my suitcase and open it to dig out the special bra and panty set I purchased just for tonight's occasion—my wedding night. Sheer white fabric and lace that cost a fortune yet consists of basically nothing.

"And put on a robe when you're finished with

your shower. Lotion up! You don't want any dry patches on your skin. If you'd like, I can come into the bathroom when you're ready and help you lotion your back," she suggests.

Ugh no. That's the last thing I want. "It's okay. I can do it."

There's another knock on the door and the back of my neck prickles with awareness.

I don't know why, but I can sense that's my future husband.

"I should get that," I start but Mother puts a hand on my arm, stopping me.

"I'll take care of it. You need to jump in the shower. Now," she says as she steers me toward the bathroom.

Reluctantly I enter the bathroom but don't quite close the door. I can hear the steady murmur of conversation between the two makeup artists. Someone's phone is ringing—it might be mine, I'm not sure. I'm straining toward the open crack of the door, wishing I could see if it's Perry who's knocking, and when I hear his deep, reassuring voice, I'm about to go to him.

"Oh no," Mother says and I can hear the displeasure in her tone. I hold my breath, waiting to see what she says. "You are the very last person who can come into this room."

"I need to talk to Charlotte," he says calmly, though I can practically feel the tension radiating off of him, filling the entire suite with his tense vibes. "Just for a moment."

"The groom is not allowed to see the bride before the ceremony! You know this," Mother chastises.

"Ma'am, that sort of thinking has been thrown out in recent years, since so many photographers like to take the wedding photos before the ceremony," one of the makeup artists says.

The room goes silent. Even Perry isn't talking.

I press my lips together to keep from laughing. I'm sure my mother did *not* appreciate that remark.

"Let me in," Perry demands, surprising me. Something heavy lands against the door and my mother yelps. I wonder if he's trying to push past her. She's pretty strong when she wants to be. "I need to know that Charlotte is all right."

My heart squeezes. He's worried about me.

"You cannot come in. And she's fine," Mother says, and I can tell she's struggling. Most likely with the door. "See you in a few hours."

The door slams, making me jump and I quickly close the bathroom door, sagging against it.

My stomach is in knots and I wish more than anything I could go to Perry and reassure him that I really am all right. There's so much I need to tell him still. About Seamus, and how he was the one I was with in Paris. That he really does mean nothing to me. Seeing him in the coffee shop left me feeling unsettled.

Even fearful.

But none of those old feelings bubbled up. Not at all. I wasn't interested. I didn't want to throw myself at Seamus and beg him to take me back. I'm over it.

Over him.

I'll be okay. I have Perry in my corner. He's about to become my husband and he cares about me. Last night only proves that. What we shared was…

Magical.

What started out as horribly fake is turning into something real.

And I can't wait to walk down the aisle toward my husband.

CHAPTER TWO

Perry

I ALMOST LOST my shit the moment Louisa Lancaster slammed the door in my face, but I restrained myself. She's my almost-mother-in-law and I'm not about to act like a dick toward her on my wedding day.

But damn it, I want to talk to Charlotte.

Now.

She sounded so frantic, so damn scared when she called me. She threw me into a full-force panic and I raced back to the hotel to be with her. All I wanted to do was hold her and tell her it was going to be okay. That's it.

Yet I couldn't get past the barrier that was her domineering mother.

What the fuck kind of weakling am I?

Checking my phone, I see I have a text from Charlotte and I send her a quick response.

Call me as soon as you get this.

I can't get over how terrified she sounded on the phone. Frantic. Breathing hard and with her voice shaking. What did this asshole do to her? Say to her? Who is he? I don't necessarily recognize the name, though I know McTiernans are part of the Morelli family. And I don't keep as close tabs on them like my brother does. He knows every single one of them by sight, even the insignificant ones.

Like the McTiernans.

They've just become more significant to me, that's for damn sure.

By the time I'm in my car and headed back to the apartment I don't even own so I can get ready for a wedding that originally wasn't of my choosing, I'm on the phone with my brother, digging for information.

"What do you think of Seamus McTiernan?" I ask the moment Winston answers.

He's quiet for a moment, as if he has to dip into the dark recesses of his deviant mind to come up with an answer.

"I don't."

That's it. That's his final answer.

"I've never even heard of this asshole," I mutter, hitting the horn when someone cuts in front of me in traffic.

"He's a quiet member of the family. From Ireland originally, though last I heard, he was living in Paris and teaching." Winston snorts. "In other words, a commoner, doing God knows what and molding impressionable young minds."

He says it with a sneer in his voice, and I almost want to laugh. Anyone who works what Winston regards as a basic job is beneath him. Like a teacher.

"He was a professor at some college," Winston continues. "Though I don't believe he works there anymore."

The lightbulb moment hits me so swiftly, I swerve my steering wheel to the right, the car veering into the next lane and nearly hitting the SUV next to me. The driver honks and gives me the finger as I speed away, irritation filling me.

Consuming me.

Seamus doing God knows what while in Paris? I could tell Winston exactly what.

That fucker was *doing* my fiancée.

Paris. Charlotte. Her mystery dark-haired lover.

Is related to the fucking Morellis.

Related to Leo Morelli, the man who punched me in the face last fucking winter at the Constantine compound. I'm supposed to put it all behind us now that my cousin Haley married him, but I will never fully trust a Morelli.

"Why are you asking about him? What does he matter?" Winston sounds bored, but I'd guess he's also curious. He once loved nothing more than to trash-talk Morellis and plot their demise. That was before he became domesticated.

I fully planned on telling Winston what I know, but I change my mind. I don't have enough details yet. I'm assuming who Seamus is to Charlotte, but I don't have all the facts. And I need them.

I need to talk to her first.

"No reason," I say, my voice casual. Like it's normal for me to bring up an obscure relation to the Morellis. "I hear he's back in town."

"He is," Winston says.

Irritation sparks. "And how do you know this?"

"I know everything that happens when it comes to the Morellis and McTiernans. I keep tabs on them at all times—you know this. Pretty sure he'll show up to your wedding reception. A bunch of them will be there," my brother explains.

If my brother knows everything about the

Morellis and McTiernans, why didn't he know about my almost-wife's involvement with one of them?

"Did you know about Charlotte and a certain Morelli relative? Specifically Seamus McTiernan? Did they have a relationship or affair or whatever the fuck?" I ask him outright.

He hesitates, and in that one single pause, I realize the asshole did know.

"Fucker," I mutter before he can say anything.

"Look, I only just found out about it, but what was the point in telling you before the ceremony?"

"You didn't tell me because you knew I'd be mad and I might walk out on this shit show of a wedding," I accuse. "He's the one, right? The man she was involved with?"

A ragged exhale leaves my brother. "Yes. They were—involved. It was short lived, she was humiliated, because he was engaged to another woman. She ran home. The end."

"The end? That's it? How long have you been sitting on this?"

"It doesn't matter."

"It does! I don't like being lied to, Winny. Even if it's supposedly for my own benefit." I'm quiet as I drive. Silently fuming.

"Are you mad?" he finally asks.

"Hell yes, I am! She fucked a Morelli!"

"Technically, he's a McTiernan."

"Morelli, McDickface, it's all the same." I blow out a harsh breath. "Something happened between the two of them this morning."

"Wait a minute. Between Charlotte and McTiernan? I need details," Winston demands.

I launch into the story, explaining to him what Charlotte told me, which wasn't much. Even though I originally told myself I wasn't going to tell my brother any of the details until I had more of them, it all comes pouring out of me anyway.

"Do you think she put that together?"

Hearing him say it out loud makes anger flare in my blood. "I don't know."

"You trust her?"

"I thought I did."

"You should ask her about it."

"Not like I can bring him up in casual conversation during our wedding reception," I mutter. "I'm still pissed you kept this from me."

"You'll get over it." Winston says it with such assuredness, because he knows it's true.

Damn it.

"And why the hell will a bunch of Morellis

and McTiernans be at my wedding reception again?" At the light, I whip my car to the right, my tires screeching on the pavement, the back end of my car squirrely.

"We're putting on a show, little brother. Uniting with the Lancasters is a fucking power move and you know it. You wedding and bedding a Lancaster makes you a king." Winston actually sounds proud, the power-hungry motherfucker.

"Start calling me king, then," I demand, my grip on the steering wheel so tight my fingers start to cramp up.

"Ha, you wish. I'm the king of this family. You're just the sorry-ass second son." He ends the call before I can say anything else, the music I was listening to before I got on the phone now flooding the interior of my car. I turn up the volume, letting the angry guitar and heavy bass beat thrum through my veins.

I should be feeling on top of the world. I'm about to marry a woman who is fine as fuck and a nice piece of ass in bed. I sound like a callous asshole even in my own thoughts, but damn. That's exactly what Charlotte is.

She's also sweet and sexy and gives me those looks—the shy glances that say so much without her uttering a word. With the big blue eyes and lush mouth and tempting body. I gave into my earlier resistance because I have every right to. She's about to become my wife.

Mine.

And no one else's.

Now I feel as if the rug has been ripped out from under my feet at the mention of a Morelli relative terrorizing her at the hotel and knowing that particular Morelli offshoot was in Paris. Just as she was.

It all adds up, and Winston just confirmed it. She fucked that guy and now he's sniffing around her, for what? Looking for another chance? I don't believe for a minute it was a coincidental meeting in a hotel coffee shop the morning of our wedding. I bet he followed her. Made sure she saw him so they could what? Engage in casual conversation? Make nice with each other and ask banal questions like, "What have you been up to?"

Please. That doesn't track.

Did she flirt with him, or did she tell that asshole to leave her alone, she's getting married? Did her heart pang at first sight of him, remembering what they shared in her past? Is she not over him? I always got that sense, but maybe I'm wrong. Pretty sure he did a number on her and it messed with her head. She's distrustful of men.

Of me.

And now he's back and possibly trying to earn a spot in her heart that he abandoned in the first place.

I punch the steering wheel and curse under my breath, full-blown anger coursing through my blood, heating it up, making me hot. I pull into the parking garage of our apartment building, reminding myself I need to calm the fuck down, but it's no use.

I'm pissed.

By the time I'm entering our apartment, I'm motivated by rage and not bothering to try and hide it. Doja Cat takes one look at me and speeds away into Charlotte's room.

Smart kitty. Not that I'd hurt Doja but I'd want to avoid me too.

Jasper makes his appearance, regal in his black suit, his hands behind his back, his expression somber as usual. The guy gives nothing away.

"Mr. Constantine. Congratulations on your wedding day," he greets.

The sour feeling in my stomach reminds me that I'm not thrilled by this. By any of it. "Jasper, I need a drink."

Jasper's expression never wavers. "Anything in particular, sir?"

Damn, I love this guy. It doesn't matter if it's not even ten in the morning—Jasper's going to hook me up with an alcoholic beverage, no questions asked. "Some of that good scotch Lancaster left behind, I think."

"Very fine choice, sir." Jasper dips his head before he makes his way to the bar. Within a minute he's standing in front of me once more, handing over the drink, which I accept with a gratefully muttered thanks.

I drain the glass of every last drop of golden liquid. It burns going down, settling in my stomach like fire and I hiss a breath in between my teeth. Jasper takes the glass without asking and pours me another.

Double this time.

I knock that one back too.

"Sir, I suggest you slow down." Jasper snatches the empty glass from my fingers, right as my phone rings. I automatically answer it, not checking who was calling.

Big mistake.

"Where are you?" It's my mother. Her voice is sharp and hushed. As if she doesn't want anyone to know she's on the phone with me. "Winston said he spoke to you almost thirty minutes ago yet you're still not here!"

Oh fuck. I was supposed to go to the compound to get ready for the wedding with my brothers. My tuxedo and everything else that goes along with it are already there, waiting for me. "I'm on my way."

"Hurry," she snaps before she ends the call.

Damn. The dragon lady has arrived, and she's breathing her fire all over me.

"I need to go, Jasper," I announce as I rise from the couch, so quickly my head swims and I nearly stumble.

"Already leaving for the wedding? Don't you need to get ready first?" Jasper asks, his tone even.

"I don't have time." I make my way to the door. I don't bother telling him where I'm getting ready. He can figure it out, I'm sure. "I need to go."

"Are you capable of driving, sir? After those two drinks?" Jasper lifts a brow.

I wave a hand. "I'll be fine."

"I'm assuming you haven't eaten anything today yet?"

"That would be correct." I snap my fingers and point at him. "Don't give me any shit, Jasper. It's my wedding day."

He ignores my statement, his expression bland. I can never get a read on this guy. "And where is Miss Charlotte?"

"At the hotel. Getting ready with her mother." I think of my beautiful wife, naked in that hotel bed, wearing only the earrings I gave her. My heart pangs and I shove the feeling aside.

My heart isn't involved in this. Not at all.

"And you're going…where?"

"Home. To Bishop's Landing."

Jasper frowns, taking a step backwards as I stride past him, heading for the door. "I thought the wedding was—"

"I'm getting ready with my family first. My brothers. A nice little bonding moment for us at the compound before we head over to the hotel where the ceremony's being held. After that, there's going to be a giant reception for like, over five hundred motherfuckers, where we can rub their faces into the fact that the Lancasters and the Constantines are now united. Maybe those Morellis will get the hint and finally back off. What do you think, Jasper? Do you know anything about your favorite Lancaster and a Morelli? Oh wait, he's not a direct Morelli. His last name is McTiernan."

I make a face, imagining what the fucker must look like. What he might mean to Charlotte. How she might never be able to forget him.

My chest aches and I rub at it absently, mentally telling myself to get over it.

Jasper's frown deepens. "I can't say that I do, no."

"That's too bad. I'm looking for information." I glance down, realizing I still have the glass clutched in my hand and I bring it to my mouth, draining the last of it. "About Charlotte and her first—love."

I choke on the last word. Did she love him?

Maybe I don't want to know.

"Sir." I glance over to find Jasper watching me with concern in his gaze. "You do realize our Miss Charlotte has had her heart broken by everyone she's ever loved."

A thread of misery courses through me at the implication of his statement.

"It would be a shame if you broke her heart too," he finishes, clamping his lips together. Almost as if he's said too much, which he sort of has.

His words make me feel like shit, when they shouldn't. I'm the one who was betrayed here. Someone's keeping secrets, and it's not me.

"I don't plan on breaking her heart," I say firmly.

And I mean it. Our hearts aren't involved in

this marriage endeavor.

"If you say so, sir." Jasper inclines his head in my direction, but I can tell.

He doesn't believe me.

That pisses me off even more.

"Well, I've gotta go, Jasper old chap." I walk up to him, slapping him on the shoulder. "I have a wedding to attend. Mine."

"I'll call Mrs. Constantine and let her know you're on your way."

"There's no need. She knows I'm coming." I shake my head and drop the glass on a nearby table, not giving a shit when I hear it fall on its side and roll onto the floor.

I'm out the door before Jasper can do or say a damn thing. By the time I'm in the parking garage, climbing into my car, I realize I've been chuckling the entire time.

It's either I laugh or fall into a complete rage. I don't know what's worse.

I pull out of the garage, the tires squealing when I turn onto the street. I don't like being made a fool of. I've endured that sort of treatment from my family for most of my life, and while it's complete bullshit and I hate it, I also tolerate it because it's my family. My brother. My mother.

I'm not going to tolerate my future wife making me look like a damn fool.

And I sure as hell am not going to let a Morelli get away with it either.

CHAPTER THREE

Charlotte

"DON'T MOVE!"

I go completely still as one of the stylists Mother hired for the day squats behind me and fluffs my train, making sure it's spread completely out across the floor. I turn my head in tiny increments, glancing over my shoulder to check the silk and lace, sucking in a breath when I see it.

The train is absolutely beautiful, trimmed in such intricate lace. The dress is gorgeous too. I feel like a queen, which was what I wanted, and now that I'm completely made up, trussed up and clutching a giant bouquet made of various flowers, including bloodred- and cream-colored roses, I'm a little in shock the moment is finally here.

"Oh my goodness, darling. You're a vision."

I glance up to find my mother watching me, her eyes filled with tears as she clutches her hands just below her chin. "Don't make me cry," I warn her, not wanting to ruin the makeup that took the artist almost two hours to apply.

When I looked in the mirror after he was through, I almost didn't recognize myself. Pretty sure Perry won't recognize me either. I look like a different person. I feel like one too.

This entire day so far has been completely surreal.

We're waiting for the ceremony to start. I'm hidden away in a tiny room made just for brides-to-be and her wedding party to stay in. I can hear the delicate strains of music playing in the gardens, coming from the string quartet Mother hired to perform. The low murmurs of conversation. People are waiting for my arrival and my stomach cramps with nerves.

I'm suddenly petrified.

"Don't cry, Charlotte." Mother dashes her fingers under her eyes, smiling when Tinsley approaches her and gives her a comforting side hug, as if she's been a part of our family her entire life.

"She's beautiful, isn't she," Tinsley says as she presses her head close to my mother's, the both of them watching me. "The dress is absolutely gorgeous, Charlotte. Perry is going to be so pleased when he sees you."

I don't say anything. Just offer her a small smile as my answer. My hands are shaking as I clutch the bouquet, the heady scent of roses drifting up, filling my senses.

Everyone is ready for the wedding ceremony, including me.

So what are we waiting for? The groom?

Oh God.

What if…what if Perry bailed? On our wedding day? What if he flat-out didn't show up? No note, no call, just poof.

Gone.

Was it because he couldn't talk to me? He could be making his own assumptions over what happened. Maybe I'm too much trouble. Too much drama. Too much…

Me.

"Hmm."

My head snaps up at the sound Caroline makes when she stops to stand beside her daughter, her gaze narrowing as she studies me with that assessing gaze. I start to sweat the longer she looks at me, and I wonder what she sees.

Wonder more if she's disappointed in her

choice of bride for her precious son. Or maybe she knows he's already left me, and she's the one who's going to tell me the wedding has been called off.

Nausea hits me, my stomach swimming. Oh God.

I think I'm going to faint.

"You're stunning," she finally proclaims and my shoulders sag with relief at her approval, which is ridiculous.

Only a few moments ago, I believed myself to be a queen, but I was wrong. I'm nothing but a mere princess. A mere lady in waiting when it comes to Caroline Constantine.

"It's almost time," the wedding planner announces as she waves her hands toward the door. "Everyone needs to get into their places! Now!"

I forget all about my worry over Perry abandoning me at the altar as we all fall into line and exit the room to wait at the entrance to the gardens. Everyone is ahead of me getting into line with me at the back. My father approaches, his expression stern, yet still handsome in his tuxedo.

"You look lovely," he offers gruffly as he stands beside me.

"Thank you." I keep my head bent, trying to fight the emotion that threatens to overtake. I don't know why I feel the sudden need to cry, but I do. This is an important moment in my life. A day I'll never forget, for all sorts of reasons.

And for whatever odd reason, I still want my father's approval. His love.

Even though deep down, I know it's a complete waste of my time.

"I want you to know..." My father's voice drifts and my gaze jerks in his direction, watching as he seems to struggle with what to say next. I tighten my arm around his, my lips falling open, ready to ask if he's all right when he finally speaks once more. "I recognize you're making a sacrifice with your life. For the family."

I'm quiet, sensing he needs to say more.

More like I *need* him to say more. To acknowledge me and what I'm doing for him.

For the Lancasters.

"And while I don't necessarily approve of Perry Constantine as your husband, I assume he won't treat you badly. He seems to have—respect for you," he continues.

His gaze finds mine and I watch him, still not speaking. The wedding planner is releasing people out into the garden. Caroline Constantine is escorted out on the arm of Winston and taken to her seat in the front row before he goes to stand beside Perry as his best man.

I hope Perry is out there. They wouldn't start this without the groom being present, would they?

Grant leads Mother out next, Finn and Crew following behind them. Only Keaton and Tinsley remain, standing directly in front of us and the nerves clamp down, making me tremble.

The moment is finally here. I'm about to walk out there and pledge my love and loyalty to Perry in front of family and strangers. I'm going to repeat my vows to him, clutch his hands in mine and promise myself to him forever.

"Just—watch out, Charlotte. The Constantines are a ruthless bunch. I know Perry seems the softest of them all, but he is still a Constantine. You won't want to cross him."

He's the one who wanted this arranged marriage. So why is he warning me?

A case of conscience? Too late for that.

"Let's go," Miranda the wedding planner murmurs to us, and I realize Tinsley and Keaton are already gone, halfway down the aisle and headed for the arbor to the strains of the delicate music playing.

Once they're in place, the music stops, and heads swivel in our direction. I steel my spine, my father's words on repeat in my brain as I take in the crowd of people. The aisle covered in deep red rose petals. The arbor where we're to be married is laden with greenery and roses as well and I keep my gaze focused on that arbor, as if I can't dare to look at the people standing beneath it.

Such as my future husband.

"Are you ready?" my father asks me.

Taking a deep breath, I nod. "Yes."

We start forward, the music launching into the wedding march. The guests rise to their feet, their expressions curious and my father squeezes my arm in his, holding me steady as he leads me to my future.

To my husband.

My feet crush the delicate petals beneath, the pointed heels of my shoes piercing them. I hear a few indrawn gasps. Whispers and soft exclamations over the beauty of my dress. It sparkles and shines, the train dragging behind me cutting through all those petals. I'm clutching my bouquet tightly, but I can still see the way the flowers tremble.

Much like my hands.

I allow my gaze to find Perry's and he's watching me, his eyes big and blue and fathomless. His hands are clutched behind his back, his posture rigid, his strong form filling the tuxedo beautifully. I remember him from earlier this morning, in my bed at the hotel. Naked and warm and affectionate.

He looks nothing like that man now. Instead, he's cold. His expression, blank.

My steps falter and my father clutches me tighter, sending me a strange look. I smile in response, not wanting him to know how rattled I am, but he can sense it.

I'm sure he can.

We stop directly in front of the pastor performing the ceremony. My father lifts my veil and folds it away from my face, as he was told to do yesterday to press a kiss to my cheek before he offers me to Perry. My fiancé steps forward, offering his arm to me and I pull away from my father, the gesture symbolic as I go to stand beside Perry.

He's quiet. He doesn't even smile in my direction and disappointment crashes through me, though I lift my chin, pretending I'm completely unaffected. We turn our heads to the pastor, who smiles kindly at us before he launches into his practiced speech. Something I've heard a hundred times already on TV shows and in movies. At other weddings I've attended in the past.

The words are familiar, but bring with them a gravity that I've not realized before. Maybe because they weren't said directly to me. I dip my head for a moment, absorbing his words, readjusting my arm that's wound around Perry's. Unexpectedly, his hand settles on top of mine, his strong fingers warm and reassuring and I glance up to find him watching me.

There's a question in his gaze, one I don't know the answer to, because I'm not sure what he's trying to communicate with me. Instead, all I can do is smile, and he does the same for me before he returns his attention to the pastor.

As do I, squaring my shoulders. The shaking stops. My heart rate slowly returns to normal as we each repeat the vows to the other as the pastor instructs. I hand my bouquet to Tinsley so I can slip the wedding ring onto Perry's finger. He then slips a band onto mine, one that is covered in large diamonds all the way around. An eternity ring.

It's stunning. Unexpected. I'm wearing the necklace he had sent over to the suite earlier this morning, along with the matching earrings he gave me last night. I am dripping in diamonds given to me by my husband, and while I know this started out as a fake wedding, I can't hide the very real feelings that are currently swarming within me.

This is an actual marriage—real and binding and true. A claiming on Perry's part. I am a Constantine now, I think as I study the ring on my finger. How it sparkles in the waning sunlight. That golden glow bathes Perry's face perfectly, gilding his cheekbones and adding an unusual light to his eyes. Eyes that are now trained on me as I hear the pastor say, "You may now kiss your bride."

Perry's hands wrap around mine and he tugs me close, his mouth finding mine in a far too brief kiss. More like a peck. I blink up at him, startled by the lack of emotion I see on his face and I part my lips, ready to whisper a question to him when the pastor announces, "Ladies and gentlemen, Mr. and Mrs. Perry Constantine."

My husband steers me so we're both facing the applauding crowd. There's not much enthusiastic cheering. It's more like polite clapping, but that's all right. I can't expect much more for a relationship that was only recently created.

The string quartet begins to play once more and Perry leads me down the aisle, a smile pasted onto his handsome face as he seemingly acknowledges everyone in attendance.

I study everyone as we walk past, smashing the rose petals into colorful bits with our shoes. The smiles on their faces as they watch us go by. Familiar family members make up some of the audience and I smile and nod in acknowledgement at my cousins. My aunts and uncles. Plenty of Lancasters turned out for this event, and I recognize a few Constantines' faces as well.

As we near the end of the aisle, I spot the wedding planner waiting for us, an anxious expression on her face. Once we're close enough, she starts talking.

"Photos, you two! We need lots of lots of photos and we must get started," Miranda says firmly as she steers us back into the small room where I waited for the ceremony only minutes before. "Let the crowd trickle out and then we'll start the session."

She shoves us into the room and shuts the door in my face before I can even utter a word. Leaving me all alone with my groom.

My husband.

Slowly I turn to face him, my train getting twisted around my legs. He's checking his phone—actually checking his phone rather than looking at me and telling me I'm the most beautiful creature he's ever seen, which I would really love to hear right about now.

"What are you doing? I ask, my voice soft. My emotions turbulent.

"Taking care of business," he answers.

He doesn't even look up from his phone. Not once.

A flicker of annoyance makes my eye twitch.

"It's our wedding day," I remind him, letting my irritation show.

"And this marriage is part of business, am I right?" His gaze lifts to mine, as if daring me to deny his statement.

I stare back at him, my throat going dry. At a complete loss over what to say.

"I have a question for you." He returns his attention to his phone once more, not waiting for my reply. "Was this meeting between you and McTiernan earlier—planned?"

I gape at him, shock coursing through my blood, chilling me to the bone. "*What?* Of course it wasn't."

"Really." His stormy gaze meets mine and I can see the doubt there. He doesn't believe me.

Will he ever?

CHAPTER FOUR

Perry

IT IS ABSOLUTE torture, continuously posing next to Charlotte, putting on a smiling face for the photographer, Susan. The same woman who took our engagement photos, and she's just as enthusiastic as the last time we were with her. She's directing the entire wedding party and our families to move here, move there, smile wider, smile brighter, look up, look down. Readjusting our positions, our poses.

It's endless.

None of it seems to bother my bride. Charlotte is absolutely serene. Calm and quiet and doing exactly what she's asked to do, no complaints, no obvious nerves showing, which is the complete opposite of her behavior when we had our engagement photos taken only what…a month ago? Six weeks?

It's astounding, the transformation.

Charlotte's posture is perfect, her skin glowing and her smile is as natural as I think I've ever seen it. As if she's happy to be doing this. Happy to finally be married to me.

While I'm over here stewing in my own shit, still confused by the sudden appearance from her supposed first lover. A man who is not-so-distantly related to the goddamn Morellis.

I can't believe he's the man she was with in Paris. The one who broke her heart and treated her like discarded trash. I wish I could ask her more questions, but it's not like I can bring it up in the middle of the photo session documenting our marriage, for Christ's sake.

The timing of his appearance is suspicious though.

After I asked if their earlier run-in was planned, we didn't bring him up again. I suppose I could've asked more questions, but I was afraid I'd get too angry. So we remained in that little room Miranda the dictator/wedding planner shoved us into while our wedding guests cleared out. We were all alone, the two of us eyeing each other warily after I was such a shit to her.

After our silent stare down, Charlotte finally asked one single question.

"Can you help me with my train?"

I, of course, assisted her with it, all the while thinking of her with another man. Kissing him. Touching him. Pressing her naked body against his. Letting him slide inside of her snug—

"Perry! Take that scowl off your face!" Susan snaps.

Realizing that I am indeed scowling, I relax my features as best I can and smile as if I haven't a care in the world while I continue to stand next to my radiant bride.

There is no denying she is absolutely beautiful today. Gorgeous. The nerves were affecting her earlier, when she walked down the aisle with her father, who didn't look pleased.

But when does he ever look pleased?

Charlotte's expression reminded me of someone who was being led to their death, and for a moment I forgot all about the asshole who showed up and focused on making Charlotte feel reassured. I touched her hand. Calmed her down.

And now I'm the one who's ragged with nerves. Exhausted and needing a drink.

Seriously, I'm looking forward to getting fucked up at the reception.

Slowly, one by one, our wedding party is set free. Until it's just me and my bride posing for photos as Susan directs us.

"Kiss her, Perry," she demands and Charlotte turns toward me, her lips parted and ready, her expression expectant.

The kiss I deliver is simple. But the spark between us ignites, just as it's done before, and unable to help myself, I kiss her again.

And again.

"Oh, that's good," Susan encourages, her shutter going off at a rapid pace. "You two are adorable."

I pull away before I lose my head, noting the dazed expression on Charlotte's face. She blinks, a faint smile curling her lips. "I thought you were mad at me."

"I'm not mad," is my immediate response, though it's a lie.

I'm definitely angry. Not at her. Not completely. More like I'm mad at the situation. At being duped. At having someone show up unexpectedly. Someone older and potentially more powerful than I am.

As in, he may have more power over Charlotte. She chose him after all, while I was assigned to her.

Big difference.

Realizing quick that Susan will never stop

photographing us, I finally put a stop to it. "We need to greet our reception guests."

The disappointment on Susan's face is clear, but she lets us go, which is a damn good thing because we're paying her, for God's sake. Taking Charlotte's hand, we leave the gardens and head down the corridor toward the ballroom where our wedding reception is taking place. My steps are hurried, Charlotte's two for my every one, and by the time we're stopped in front of the closed double doors where the party is happening, Charlotte is out of breath, her breasts rising and falling with her every inhale and exhale.

I notice this, of course. Every piece of her intrigues me, and I think of her—yet again—naked and flushed and eager for me to be inside of her. I'd hoped for a repeat performance tonight. I may not have been on board for all of this marriage stuff at first, but now that we're here, I deserve to take advantage of the perks to being married.

As in, having sex with this very sexy, desirable woman.

Again.

"Do I look all right?" she asks as she turns toward me.

She looks fucking perfect.

"You look fine," I tell her instead, and I see the vague disappointment in her gaze.

Damn it, I don't want to lay it on too thick. What if she's already considering the many ways she could possibly escape our marriage? Escape me?

And what if she's lying? This could all be a big show for my benefit—and our families. She acts like an innocent, virginal bride but we know the truth. She claims she wants to get away from her father, and I know he's an asshole, but is she a willing participant in this game her family is playing with mine?

I suppose I could be nicer. Lay on the charm and encourage her that she wants to be with me instead of acting cold and indifferent. It's our wedding day, for Christ's sake. What the fuck is wrong with me?

Since when do I give in so easily?

I'm a Constantine, damn it. Enough with the pity party.

A shaky exhale leaves her and she waves her hands, as if her palms are sweaty. "Okay. Let's do this."

She's about to reach for the door handle but I grab hold of her waist, pulling her to me before I viciously kiss her. Claim her. Remind her that I'm the one she was with last night. I'm the one whose diamonds she's wearing.

I'm the one who gave her that ring on her finger.

We break away from each other at the same time, the both of us breathing heavily. Reaching out, she brushes her finger against the corner of my lips. "My lipstick," she murmurs, showing me her fingertip that's colored with the soft pink hue.

"Marked me," I whisper, smiling at her. "Let's go, wife."

Pleasure suffuses her face and I reach past her, opening the door. There's a man in a suit standing guard, and the moment he spots us, he lifts the microphone he was clutching in his hand and switches it on.

"Ladies and gentlemen, our special guests have finally arrived! Mr. and Mrs. Perry Constantine!"

There is cheering and laughter and glasses being raised in our honor when our guests spot us. I can feel the love and warmth buzzing in this room—and it's all for me. For Charlotte.

For us.

I also notice the familiar faces mixed among the strangers. Family and friends and business associates. It feels like everyone from the Halcyon offices is here. All of my siblings and their significant others. There are Lancasters there as well, I recognize them thanks to their icy stares and regal expressions.

"Ready to do this?" I ask her.

Her smile is soft, as is the glow in her eyes. "Yes. Let's go greet our guests."

✧ ✧ ✧

IT WAS EXHAUSTING, talking to everyone who's at the wedding reception, and finally we get a break and are sitting at our table, surrounded by our wedding party, which is actually quite small. My brothers and their women accompany them, as well as Charlotte's brothers. Grant actually has a girlfriend—who would tolerate that asshole—and she seems quite taken with him as they snuggle close together at the table, just on the other side of Charlotte.

My wife has already had two full glasses of champagne and not much dinner, but I'm not going to tell her what to do.

Hell, I'm a few drinks in myself. I need to withstand the barrage of questions that have been thrown at us since we walked into the gorgeously decorated ballroom. The Lancasters spared no expense. There are flowers everywhere—fucking every available open spot you see is covered with rich dark flowers. The room is heady with their rich scent.

There are lights strung everywhere, dripping from the ceiling in long ropes. Candles and candelabra scattered all over the tables, their gentle light flickering. The food is rich, the alcohol is flowing and the chandeliers above twinkle and shine down upon us. Like we're living a goddamn fairy tale.

I'm enjoying it, I can't lie, but I'm also waiting for the pretense to fall, so to speak. There are Morellis here, beyond the ones involved with our family directly. I recognize their faces. Their dark hair and black, soulless eyes. Their arrogant airs and fake smiles. I'm on guard, waiting for a particular relative of theirs to show his face. To reveal himself to me and my bride.

But so far, there is no sign of Seamus McTiernan anywhere.

"You look ready to cut a bitch," Winston says as he pulls his chair closer to mine. I'm guessing he's in the mood for conversation. "And I'm not talking about your beautiful bride, either."

"No, I definitely don't want to cut her," I agree, my gaze sweeping the room as I clutch my drink glass with my fingertips.

"Looking for someone in particular?" Winston

lifts his brows in question.

"Don't say his name out loud." I send him a death look, quickly glancing over at Charlotte to make sure she didn't hear us. She's too engaged in conversation with Grant's saintly girlfriend to notice us.

"Is he here?" I ask my brother. "Because if he is, I'd like to personally escort him the fuck out."

Winston chuckles. "Look at you, getting all territorial over a woman you barely know."

"I know her well enough," I tell him. "And she's my wife now. No one touches what's mine."

"I haven't seen him," my brother says, glancing around the room, his expression impassive. "There are plenty of Morellis here though. Even a couple of McTiernans."

"I'll rip his face off if he shows up and even tries to talk to my wife," I practically snarl before bringing my glass to my lips and draining the last of it.

"He might make an appearance." Winston sounds amused. As if he wants to see me get violent on my wedding day. "I wouldn't put it past him."

"He's a ballsy son of a bitch, then," I mutter, wishing I had another drink.

"Just like the rest of the Morelli clan." Winston's lips tip up in a barely there smile. "You and the wifey good?"

"Wifey?" I raise a brow, sending a quick glance in Charlotte's direction before I return my attention to my brother. "We're all right."

"You seemed pissed at the altar."

"Felt a little tense. Not gonna lie." My expression turns grim. I can literally feel it transform. "Didn't help, what happened earlier this morning."

"Hey. I'm sorry I didn't tell you earlier. About your wife and—McTiernan," Winston says, genuine sympathy in his gaze.

I shrug a shoulder, trying to act like it's no big deal, but I'm still pissed. And surprised my brother would apologize. That's not like him. "It's whatever. I'm still stuck on the fact that he magically appeared. His timing is just…too close to our wedding. She sees him literally the morning of the day we're getting married? How coincidental is that?"

"I'll do a little digging," Winston says, his expression turning thoughtful. "See what I can come up with in regards to this Seamus asshole. Look into his professional and personal life."

"I'd appreciate it." Relief hits me. As does the realization that I'm very, very grateful for my brother and his shady-ass skillset right now. "You'll report back to me as soon as you know?"

"Aren't you going on a honeymoon?"

I shake my head. "We didn't plan anything."

"Oh. Right." Winston smothers the smile that's trying to appear with a swipe of his hand. "Okay. That's unfortunate."

Huh. I think he's hiding something, but I'm not questioning it.

CHAPTER FIVE

Charlotte

I'M DRUNK.

Drunk at my own wedding reception. Basking in the love and attention that's being thrust upon me. Our guests' words of congratulations fill me with a fizzy happiness that reminds me of the bubbles in my champagne glass. Their admiring tone when they compliment my dress, my hair, my flowers, makes me smile uncontrollably. I'm happy.

Legitimately happy for what feels like the first time in a while.

Or maybe it's all the alcohol I'm consuming. Nonstop champagne. I can't stop drinking it. I tried to eat earlier but my stomach cramped, and I felt too nervous. The vibe my husband is giving off is...

Unsettling.

He's not happy and I don't know exactly why. He's also acting closed off, and I wonder what I did to make him angry. We haven't been able to talk about my seeing Seamus this morning, and I'm sure that has something to do with his shift in mood.

I try not to let it bother me.

After the speeches were given—one by my mother who started crying in the middle of it and made me cry, and the other from Winston who said wonderful and sometimes vulgar things about his brother—I moved from table to table, trying to speak with everyone I know. I visited with my cousins. Whit was there with his fiancée, Summer, and they're blissfully in love. He keeps a hand on her at all times, as if he never wants to stop touching her.

I wonder what that's like, experiencing a love like that. Having a man so enraptured with you, he doesn't ever want you out of his sight.

I chat with Whit's sisters Sylvie and Carolina. They're both beautiful, with similar features and the Lancaster icy blue eyes, the both of them bright blonde like me. We could all pass as sisters, we look so much alike.

But I'm nothing like them. Not really. Sylvie is manic, her pupils large, her mannerisms unusual. She used to be obsessed with death, which scared me when I was younger. Carolina is more reserved and doesn't say much. I've always felt as if we have more in common than any of my other cousins.

"Hey."

I turn to find my younger brother, Crew, standing in front of me, handsome in his tux and looking so grown up. He just turned eighteen only last month and there's always this undercurrent of tension running through him, just beneath his skin. As if he's pissed at the world and wants to take all of his anger out on it.

Which I suppose I can't blame him. It seems to be a toxic trait among Lancaster men—their anger. They all have it. Every generation. My father and uncles, they're all mad as hell. Whit used to be a nightmare, until eventually his wife calmed him down some. Grant was terrible, though he seems a tad sweeter now thanks to his girlfriend, Alyssa.

Only a tad though.

"Hi." I smile and practically throw myself at Crew, closing my eyes and pressing my cheek to the lapel of his jacket when he gives me a lingering squeeze. We are not an affectionate family either, but Crew and I were close when we were younger. I considered him my best friend at one point, though I never knew exactly how he felt about me.

Which is fine. He grew distant as he got older, but I understood why. Our father isn't one to encourage close relationships among his children. He probably didn't want Crew to get soft by spending too much time with me.

Ridiculous and awful, but true. And us Lancasters—especially the males—are expected to do what their fathers say, no questions asked.

"You seem happy, Charlotte," he says once we pull away from each other. "Is that Perry dude treating you okay?"

"That Perry dude is my husband, and yes, he's treating me just fine." I smile, swaying toward my brother and he slings his arm around my shoulders, tucking me close to his side. "The ceremony was beautiful, don't you think?"

"It was nice. And this is quite the party." He glances down at me, affection filling his gaze. "I'm really happy for you, but just…be careful, okay?"

I frown. "Be careful of what?"

"Your husband. Your new in-laws. All of it. You don't know them. Not really," he reminds me. "And while they might seem like they're going to welcome you into the family, you need to keep your guard up. Don't trust them."

He's right. I know he is. But that's the last thing I want to hear on my wedding day. "I'll be fine."

"I hope so." His smile is almost pained. "You lead too much with your heart, when you should be protecting it at all costs. It's your best and worst quality. Look what happened the last time you surrendered your heart to someone. It got stomped on."

I blink at him, hating the reminder. Hating worse that it came from the one brother I trust more than the others, though maybe he's the only one who'll be completely honest with me. "I'm not in love with him, Crew."

"Yet you married him."

"Because I was bartered off to him." I lower my voice. "I didn't have a choice."

"Right, so don't look at him with stars in your eyes or whatever the fuck." He scowls, seemingly irritated he would even say such a thing. "Keep your walls up. Don't let him—them—hurt you."

I part my lips, automatically ready to defend the Constantines when I'm interrupted.

"Hey, everyone! It's time for Perry and Charlotte to have their first dance as a married couple!" the DJ suddenly announces.

I pull away from Crew, grateful for the distraction. "I need to go."

"You're throwing yourself completely into this wedding bullshit, aren't you?" The gleam in his eyes tells me he's not impressed.

He probably thinks I'm an idiot.

Well, what am I supposed to do? At least I'm out from under my father's control once and for all.

"Yes." I lift my chin. "I am."

I turn away from Crew before he can say anything else and pick up my skirts, hurrying toward the dance floor. I spot Perry standing by the DJ booth, his gaze alighting on mine when he spots me, a flickering of irritation in his eyes.

I'm sure he's over the wedding bullshit as Crew called it, too. Well, too bad.

We have a part to play, and our roles aren't over yet.

I stop directly in front of Perry, and without a word, he sweeps me into his arms, just as the song begins to play. It's something slow and old and terribly romantic and I could easily find myself falling into the moment. Believing it with every fiber of my being.

But something holds me back. Crew's words are on repeat in my brain. Reminding me I shouldn't trust Perry or the Constantines in general.

The only person I can count on is myself.

We're quiet as we move about the dance floor and I turn my face when Susan's flash momentarily blinds me. Perry tightens his grip around my waist, his movements surprisingly smooth. Impressive. The man can dance.

Of course, I don't know him that well, so everything I discover still feels like a surprise.

"Are you having fun?" he asks when we're about a third into the song.

"The reception is beautiful, yes," I tell him, keeping my head bent.

"Charlotte." His voice is firm, causing me to glance up at him. "Are you afraid to look at me?"

I slowly shake my head. "No."

My voice is shaky. I don't know why I'm suddenly filled with fear. He's never given me a reason to be scared before.

"Good." His expression is smug. "I need you to explain something to me."

"What?" I ask weakly.

"Who Seamus McTiernan is to you." Perry spins me in a quick circle, shocking me. "You never really said."

"Oh." I swallow hard, wishing I didn't have to

talk about Seamus while having my first dance with my husband.

"That's all you have to say about him? *Oh?*" He catches my gaze with his and I see it now. The turbulence in the blue depths of his eyes. "Would you rather not tell me?"

I press my lips together, wishing I could tell him yes. It would be so much easier if I never had to explain myself. Never had to admit that Seamus was my instructor. My crush. My first real relationship with a man.

"It's that bad, isn't it," Perry continues, his voice a low, deep rumble. "Whatever he did to you. Whoever he was to you. It's so bad, you don't want to say it out loud."

"It was before you," I start and he laughs.

Actually laughs.

"Whatever happened before me, during me, after me, it doesn't matter. Right, Char? Since this is nothing but a charade?" He spins me around again, his movements smooth and elegant and throwing me completely off. He's so angry, yet you'd never know it to look at him. "Did you ask him to come here? To interrupt your wedding? To put a stop to it?"

Icy tendrils of dread slither down my spine and I slow my steps, gaping at him. This angry yet controlled man who is my husband. Oh he's furious. I can see the emotion flicker in his gaze. The tension radiates throughout his body and another realization hits me.

He's not just angry. Maybe he's also…

Jealous?

"I didn't reach out to him," I admit, needing him to know the truth. "I haven't talked to him since I was in Paris. Before he—"

"Broke your heart?" Perry finishes for me. "Funny how the man you fell madly in love with shows up on our wedding day."

"Are you implying I had something to do with it? Is that why you've been so cold toward me all day?"

"What did you expect, Charlotte? How am I supposed to act? You're making a damn fool of me."

"I'm no—"

He cuts me off. "Besides, none of this is real anyway. Remember?"

I come to a complete stop. So does Perry.

As does the song.

"The father-daughter dance is next! Reggie Lancaster, come on out and dance with your beautiful daughter!"

I wince at the DJ's announcement, gasping

when Perry let's go of me as if he can't wait to get rid of me. I watch in disbelief as he takes a couple of steps backward, his gaze still on mine, his lips tight with fury.

Almost as if he wants to be disappointed in me. Like he expects my traitorous act.

My father appears, handsome in his tuxedo, holding his arms out to me and I go to him, letting him embrace me as another slow song starts. He's just as smooth a dancer as Perry, saying all the right things, just loud enough for our guests sitting close to the dance floor to hear. Like how proud he is of me. How beautiful I look and how wonderful the reception has been. Putting on the proper performance of a loving, proud father.

I nod and offer my simple replies, my gaze snagging on Perry, who's watching us carefully, as if he'll launch into action and separate us if need be. He hates my father, and while I'm worried over Perry's earlier accusations, I know no matter what, he'll protect me.

Knowing that gives me an inkling of faith. Just about the only faith I have right now.

"I have a question."

My father glances down at me, his brows furrowed. "What is it?"

"Did you invite…" My voice drifts and I swallow hard. "Seamus McTiernan?"

He actually snorts, shaking his head. "Why in the world would I do that? I despise that man. He helped ruin your reputation."

"It's just—" I clamp my lips shut, not about to admit to my father I saw Seamus this morning. He'd surely go into a rage, and probably blame me for it.

My gaze finds Perry's yet again and he flicks his chin at me. A silent question if I'm all right. I offer a quick smile before my gaze slides from my husband to another man behind him, his face in shadow. The breadth of his shoulders, the way he holds himself is familiar and I stiffen in my father's arms, all the air clogging my throat when the man shifts out of the shadows to reveal himself.

Seamus.

At my wedding reception.

Standing just behind my husband.

CHAPTER SIX

Perry

I DON'T TEAR my eyes off of Charlotte dancing with her father, noting how uncomfortable she seems, and how perfectly natural he acts. Smiling down at her as he steers her across the dance floor, his lips moving. Probably saying nice things about his daughter that he doesn't really mean.

It's all about appearances for the Lancasters, which I get.

It's the same for the Constantines as well.

My wife and I are the culmination of that thought process, and it's fucking painful, how they put us through this charade, all for them to look good to others. A fake marriage, a fake life. I wanted more.

I deserve more. Charlotte does too. And maybe we can have it…

If I so much as see Reggie Lancaster's fingers

barely squeeze her arm, I'm on him. I don't care who sees me take down my father-in-law at the damn wedding reception. He has no right to intimidate or hurt her, especially now.

She's mine, whether he likes it or not.

The father-daughter dance seems to go smoothly, the façade maintained until near the end of the song, when Charlotte's eyes go wide and she slows her steps. Our gazes had just locked, but now she's staring beyond me.

At someone else.

I glance over my shoulder in the direction she's looking, spotting the man I ran into in the hotel lobby yesterday afternoon before the rehearsal.

The man who I thought looked familiar.

The man who's currently staring at my bride as if she's a tasty morsel he can't wait to get his mouth on.

"Hey." I turn to face him, letting my blatant hostility show. "Do I know you?"

His expression is downright amused as he contemplates me. "You're the groom."

I stand up taller. "You didn't answer me. Are you an invited guest?"

There's a hush that comes over the guests sitting at the tables nearby, but I don't give a shit.

"She's a good one, your bride. Watch out for her." His accent is thick. Irish but touched with something else. "Before someone else possibly snags her up."

His comment reminds me of the random texts I received from an unknown number—what was it, a week ago? I sort of forgot about them.

Until now.

Could Seamus have been the one to send them to me?

I take a step forward, my focus now one hundred percent on him. I'm assuming I know who he is, but I don't want him to realize it. Not yet. "Who the hell says that to a groom on his wedding day?"

"A man who's been—intimate with said groom's bride, that's who." The smirk appears and I see red.

Seamus.

I don't even think. I just react, lunging for him and plowing my fist into his smug, shitty mouth, not holding back. I put all of my strength into that hit and it knocks him back so hard he stumbles, landing on the floor among the gasps and horrified shrieks that fill the ballroom.

The music switches off. I hear my father-in-law shout, "What the hell is going on here?"

Seamus touches the side of his mouth lightly as I stand over him with clenched fists, his dark gaze on mine, burning with intensity. "Nice right hook you got there."

"Get the fuck out of here," I demand. "*Now.*"

"I'm a guest of the bride's—" he starts and I bellow in murderous rage, ready to kick the shit out of him when I feel an arm band around my middle, strong as steel.

"He's not worth it," Winston mutters in my ear as he holds me back from the taunting fucker. "Let security take care of him."

Out of nowhere two burly bald dudes appear, dressed in matching black suits and with sunglasses covering their eyes, despite the party being indoors. They each grab hold of Seamus's upper arms and jerk him into a standing position.

I glare at him, Winston still holding me back, noting the trickle of blood at the corner of Seamus's mouth. My knuckles throb from the intensity of the punch and I wish I'd done more noticeable damage. It would've given me great satisfaction, to see him hurt. Suffering.

"Escort him out, please," Winston snaps at the bodyguards and Seamus chuckles, shaking his head as the two men turn him around, supporting him like a sack of potatoes as they lead him toward the exit.

"Did she tell you about me? Did she?" Seamus calls out, still chuckling as the bodyguards drag him away.

I don't answer him. Neither does Winston. Within seconds, the man I assume is Seamus McTiernan is gone, and Winston is loosening his grip on me. I shake off his hands, glancing around at everyone watching us with shocked expressions on their faces. The entire room is silent, enthralled with our little performance, and I can literally feel Charlotte's gaze boring into my back. I'm sure she's…what?

Disappointed? I made a fucking scene at our wedding reception, but what else was I supposed to do?

Maybe she was glad to see that asshole show up. Maybe she planned all of this and hoped he'd make a public spectacle to make me look like the asshole.

Fuck, I can barely stand the idea of that. Earlier today I was so hyper focused on the woman I spent time with last night. She was all I could think about. The woman I took to bed, who I fucked. Thoroughly. God, she'd been vulnerable and so damn sexy I blew my wad way too quickly, like a fucking novice.

I'd fully planned on having a wild night of sex with my bride later this evening, where I could linger over her delectable body. I would've taken my time with her. Make her come again and again until she was begging for it.

Begging for me.

We deserve a night like that. After everything we've put up with and been through over the last six weeks. We're compatible. Last night more than proved that.

But then this morning had to happen and threw everything off. The panic in her voice when she called me still sends a spike of ice-cold fear spreading through my gut just thinking about it.

This dick actually showing up on my god-damn wedding day has complicated matters considerably. And that's an understatement.

"Jesus," I hear Winston mutter before he signals to the DJ. The music starts back up, a fast number to get everyone onto the dance floor, which works.

"Well, that was certainly unexpected," Reggie Lancaster mutters as he walks off, abandoning Charlotte completely.

Typical.

My gaze finds hers and she watches me, her teeth sinking into her lower lip, those clear blue eyes now shrouded with worry. Without hesitation I go to her, startled when I get close enough that she grabs my hand, the one I socked Seamus in the mouth with, and she does the craziest fuckin' thing.

She brings my hand up to her mouth and presses a gentle kiss to my throbbing knuckles. Then another one. And yet another one, her hands gently cradling mine, her gaze never straying from me.

The apology is there in her eyes and I refuse to start an argument with my wife in the middle of our wedding reception. I pull her into my arms and dip my head, kissing her soundly, pleased to hear the hoots and hollers of our wedding guests as they voice their approval.

"Guess it's not a real party until there's a fight, am I right?" asks the DJ.

The crowd cheers in answer as they spill onto the dance floor.

I take Charlotte's hand and lead her off. Away from the crowds, until I find a dark spot in the farthest corner of the ballroom, away from everyone and everything else. It's just the two of us tucked away where no one can see us. The music is loud and I press her against the wall, my face nuzzling hers as I whisper in her ear.

"That was him, wasn't it?" I pause, letting my words sink in. "The man you were with in Paris. The one who broke your heart."

She's hesitant for a moment before she slowly nods, her hair brushing against my cheek. "I wanted to explain everything but didn't know how, especially now. During the reception. And the wedding. It was never the appropriate time."

Valid point. When is there ever an appropriate time to bring up your former lover making an appearance on your wedding day?

"You knew he'd be here." It's a statement, not a question because I believe she knew all along he'd show his face here.

I do.

God, the scent of her is doing something to me. Making my dick hard, for one. I need to focus, but having her so close, despite the many layers of her dress and how she's trussed up in some corset thing that looks impossible to take off, I can feel her curvy body. The heat of her. Her soft hair. Her lush mouth and dewy skin and those damn Constantine diamonds glittering in her ears, around her neck.

She's gorgeous. And she's legally all mine.

"No, of course not," she breathes, her warm breath wafting across my face. "I had no idea he would show up. None."

"You saw him before though." My voice is tight, tense with anger. "Yesterday. Here."

When I saw him yesterday in the lobby—had he just left Charlotte? Had they spoke before the wedding rehearsal? I remember the smug expression on his face. As if he knew a secret.

"No..."

"Tell me, Charlotte." My hands are firm when they land on her waist, giving her a gentle shake as I slowly pull away from her so I can look into her eyes. "He was in the hotel lobby when I arrived late for the rehearsal. I ran into him."

And all along I'm sure that prick knew exactly who I was, while I was the idiot who had no clue.

I feel stupid.

Worse? I feel played.

She frowns, her delicate brows drawing together. "You saw Seamus yesterday?"

I hate the way she says his name. The easy familiarity of it.

"Yes," I bite out. "He was here, lurking around. Probably waiting for me."

After meeting with you?

The unspoken words hang between us.

Nothing about yesterday's interaction with him in the lobby feels accidental. Not now, when

I know the truth.

A soft exhale escapes her and she closes her eyes, her plump lips parted. "I don't know what he's doing. Or why he's here."

"You so sure about that?"

My sharp tone causes her eyes to flash open and she glares. "What, you don't believe me?"

"No, I don't." The words fall from my lips without hesitation, and for one hot moment, I regret them.

She glares at me. Beautiful and devastated after her husband tells her he doesn't believe her on their wedding day.

Great way to kick off the marriage.

"And here I thought you were different." Her voice is flat, devoid of any emotion.

I frown. "What the hell are you talking about?"

Remaining quiet, her eyes narrow and she reaches out, her hands planting on my chest and giving me a worthy shove.

Worthy enough that I take a couple of steps backwards, allowing her to escape.

I watch her go, irritation flaring in my blood. In my mind. This woman…

I want to trust her.

But I don't know if I can.

CHAPTER SEVEN

Charlotte

I'M EXHAUSTED.

A wedding is absolutely draining. All the planning and anticipation and dread. All the worry and nervousness and excitement. I've been running on empty all day long, and now that I'm standing in the elevator with Perry while we ride up to the penthouse suite, where we'll be spending our first night together as husband and wife, I feel like I could fall asleep standing up.

I press my head against the mirrored wall, closing my eyes. The wedding gown is heavy, like the mental weight I'm currently dealing with. Perry stands just in front of me, and when I open my eyes, I can see his face in the reflection of the mirror. The tightness around his mouth. The strain at the corner of his eyes.

He's stressed. Mad. All because of me.

"I didn't know he would show up." I don't need to clarify who *he* is. Perry knows who I'm talking about.

My husband's gaze meets mine in the mirrored walls. "You keep saying that, yet I still don't believe you."

Breathing deeply, I close my eyes once more, giving up. Why should he believe me? It doesn't look good, Seamus attending our reception. I know it doesn't. Perry and I barely know each other, though I thought we were learning to trust each other…

"Doesn't stop me from wanting to fuck you on our wedding night though," Perry continues.

My eyes pop open to find him still watching me in the mirror's reflection. I see hunger in his gaze now, and my traitorous body responds, my blood humming and my skin tingling as it remembers how good it was between us last night.

"You going to stop me?" He lifts his brows in challenge.

Ugh, he's too handsome when he looks at me like that. He got rid of the bow tie sometime during the reception and the first couple of buttons of his shirt are undone, exposing the smooth column of his throat. I remember kissing him there. How warm his skin is. The groan that sounded low in his throat—

"Are you?" he asks, interrupting my thoughts.

A ding sounds and the doors slide open, me hurrying out of the elevator without a word. Perry follows silently alongside me, magically producing a key card from the pocket of his tuxedo jacket. I don't know where he got it.

I don't bother asking either.

Within seconds the door is open and we're entering the suite, the click of the door shutting loud in the otherwise hushed silence.

Pressing my hand to the wall, I kick off my shoes, a soft exhale of relief escaping. They were killing me. I'm not used to being in heels for that long.

Perry walks past me, still silent, coming to a sudden stop with a muttered curse. I go to him, stopping right beside him when I see what he's staring at.

The king-sized bed is covered in deep red rose petals. Formed in the shape of a heart.

He turns to me, his expression grim. "Did you request this?"

I slowly shake my head. "Of course not."

His scowl deepens. "Right. Not an ounce of romance is involved in this marriage."

The silence in the room is deafening and I

take a deep breath, trying to find the strength to be honest with him.

"Why are you being so cruel?" I whisper, hating how weak I sound. I should be stronger. While some of this is my fault—yes, I was involved with Seamus—but I never asked him to come to the wedding. I have no control over that man. After everything that happened in Paris, I assumed I'd never see his face again.

Perry blows out a harsh breath and without thought I reach for the diamond necklace I'm wearing, my fingers tracing over the stones. He notices, his gaze darkening and he lifts it to mine. "That asshole showing up to our reception looked really fucking bad, Charlotte."

His words are like a knife. Multiple stab wounds to my stupidly tender heart. "Trust me. I know—"

He interrupts me, his voice flat. "No, I don't think you do. I'm starting to think you wanted him there."

"I already told you—"

"I don't care what you say. Actions speak louder than words." Perry's eyes blaze with anger. "If you wanted to be with him, why didn't you tell me? We would've never had to go through that stupid ceremony if you'd just been truthful with me in the first place."

"I don't want to be with him!" The words blast out of me, so loudly, Perry flinches.

He watches me, that wary expression on his handsome face. But he doesn't say a word.

I look away from him, staring at that stupid rose-petal heart on the bed, swallowing down the sudden swamp of emotion that threatens to take over me. "I suppose I can't change your mind."

"Tonight, you sure as hell can't." I return my attention to him to find he's undoing a few buttons on his shirt. "That's not how I expected the evening to go."

"Me either," I admit with a whisper.

"Think it'll hit the gossip rags?" When I frown, he continues. "Me knocking out your former lover. I'm sure someone caught a photo of it."

I wince at his choice of words, trying to fight the worry that threatens. My father won't be pleased if that comes out. I'm sure he'll blame me for it happening too. "I don't know. I hope not."

"Same. My family will *not* be pleased." He strides toward me, making me suck in a surprised breath when he reaches over, his body brushing against mine when he plucks something off the bed.

An envelope with the words *Mr. and Mrs. Perry Constantine* written across it.

Without asking he tears into it, frowning as he reads what's written on the thick, cream-colored card. "Oh fuck me."

"What is it?" I take the offered card from him to see that it's describing our gift from his brother, Winston.

An all-expenses-paid trip to Mexico for five days. We don't have to worry about packing our bags and preparing anything. It's all been taken care of for us by Winston. Our honeymoon that we never thought to plan. There's even a little itinerary where it states we leave tomorrow morning.

It sounds like a dream. A chance to get away from everyone and everything. To get to know my husband and spend more time with him. All alone.

"I'm not going," Perry announces, crushing my already shattered heart.

"Perry." I turn toward him, attempting to reach for him but he dodges away from me, shedding his jacket and dropping it onto a nearby chair. "I don't understand why you're so angry with me."

"I already told you why. This isn't how I

imagined my wedding day to be." He undoes the cufflinks at his wrists and my entire body goes warm.

My husband is slowly undressing in front of me while also totally furious with me, and like the sick, love-starved girl I am, that hot ribbon of arousal unfurls deep within my body. Making me yearn.

For him.

"He *broke* my heart. I haven't seen him since I left Paris and that was over a year ago. Why would I want him here on our wedding day? I was so shocked, seeing him this morning. When he approached me in the coffee shop, he—he threatened me, Perry."

He frowns, the displeasure on his face obvious. "*Threatened* you? How?"

I think of what Seamus told me. How my fiancé isn't what he seems. How he comes from a family that will destroy whatever and whoever they need to in order to get what they want.

I said so to Seamus and I still feel it now—there is comfort in that. Knowing that Perry's family is so very similar to mine. And while it might not be right, it's all I know and those sorts of things don't scare me.

Even though they probably should.

"Charlotte." Perry's stern voice pulls me from my thoughts. "How exactly did he threaten you?"

"He—he said you have something he wants," I admit. "And that he plans on collecting soon."

"Referring to you, I assume?" Perry raises a brow.

Just like Seamus did.

I nod, dropping my gaze so I can study my hands, which are completely twisted together. "He scared me, and I think that was his goal. He wanted me frightened and worried about his next move. Why, I'm not sure. When I left Paris—things were left unsaid. It's not like we had an actual breakup or even a conversation. Maybe—maybe he just wants to talk to me."

"You're not that naïve, Charlotte. I know you don't believe he showed up out of nowhere on our wedding day hoping you two can just talk," Perry says.

He's right. But what could Seamus want from me now, after all of this time? He's missed his chance. If he really wanted to break up our impending marriage, he had plenty of opportunity leading up to this moment. Our engagement was announced weeks ago. Why didn't he come running then?

Perry's deep voice seeps into my brain, interrupting my thoughts.

"Would you have run away with him if he asked you to this morning?"

"No." I shake my head. Not at all.

"What about at the beginning? When this entire fraud first started?"

I hesitate, my mind flooded with thoughts. Memories.

"And there's my answer," he says quietly.

My gaze goes to his, noting the displeasure on his face, and I look away quickly. I don't bother denying it, because he's right.

I might've listened to Seamus then. I might've—oh this pains me to think—run away with him if he asked. I didn't know Perry at all. The arranged marriage was a way out for me. To get away from my father once and for all. It didn't matter if I loved the man I was marrying or not.

If Seamus had shown up that early in the game, I would've gone with him. I know I would've.

But now?

I wouldn't.

I can't.

A ragged exhale leaves Perry but he doesn't say anything else, and when I finally dare to look up at him, I find that he's moved even closer to me, all the anger gone from his expression.

Now he just looks as tired as I feel.

"You need help out of that dress?" he asks, and not in a sexy way.

Which is fine. I don't expect him to want to have sex with me tonight, not after everything that happened at the reception.

I nod my answer.

"Turn around," he commands gently and I do as he says, sucking in a quiet breath when he begins to undo the many buttons that line the length of my spine. The fabric parts as he continues to work, his warm fingers brushing against my back and I try to suppress the shiver that wants to steal over me but it's no use.

And he feels it. He pauses for a moment and I go completely still, wondering what he's going to do next.

My husband doesn't disappoint. He draws his finger along my spine, starting between my shoulder blades, his touch so light, I can almost believe he's not touching me at all.

But he is, and that gives me…so much hope.

Too much.

"Fuck, Charlotte." He sounds pained. Tortured. The last button is undone and then he's pushing the gown off of me, until it falls in a heap around my feet, the frothy skirt tall enough to reach my knees. "Look at you."

I'm wearing the white lacy strapless bra and matching panties—well, really, it's a thong. My entire ass is bared and he's currently staring at it. I can feel his eyes on me, heavy and hot. I want him to see me like this. I'm his wife now.

I want him to treat me like one. As if I'm his.

And no one else's.

"Help me out of the dress, Perry," I say with a confidence I don't actually feel. He grabs hold of my upper arm, stabilizing me as I try to step out and over the pile of fabric that is my wedding gown, but I nearly fall over.

He catches me before I do. Wraps his arms around my waist from behind and completely lifts me up, making me squeal. He kicks the dress out of his way before he deposits me back onto the floor. I'm about to turn and face him but he doesn't give me the chance, moving far too quickly. His hands find my waist once more and then he's pushing me, sending me toppling onto the bed, where I land on my stomach in the middle of the rose petals.

I try to turn around yet again but he's on me, pressing my body into the mattress, the scent of roses surrounding me, the petals sticking to my skin. I turn my face to the side, my cheek resting on the bed, and I close my eyes when I feel his big, hot body wrap all around me, holding me in place.

"I shouldn't do this," he mutters and I wonder if he's talking to me or to himself. "I shouldn't."

I don't speak, afraid I'll say the wrong thing. Worried I'll snap him out of whatever spell he's currently under that has him wrecked over me.

Wrecked in the best possible way.

A soft moan leaves me when he begins to kiss my back, his lips following the ridges of my spine. I arch upwards with my hips, my ass nudging against his front and I can feel his erection.

He's already hard for me, and that sends a heady thrill spiraling.

"Damn it." He sounds angry but the emotion doesn't scare me. His touch, his mouth is soft yet firm, and everything inside of me tightens with anticipation.

What will he do next?

When he pulls away, the crash of disappointment is almost my undoing. My muscles tighten and I brace myself for more cruel words of rejection. He's so angry, so frustrated with me and everything that happened. Even though I had nothing to do with it, he still blames me, and I suppose he's right in wanting to do so.

None of this would've ever happened if I hadn't had an affair with my instructor in Paris. If I hadn't had my stupid dreams of being an architect or studying European architectural history. I'd only wanted to stretch my wings and try something different. Something for myself.

Instead, I practically ruined my life and fell for the wrong person. If I'd only known who Seamus was related to back then, and who I'd be paired with now…

I would've never done it.

The realization smacks me in the chest, making my heart ache. I want to be with Perry. Despite everything we've been through, despite how our relationship started in the first place, I want him to give me a chance. I want us to give each other a chance.

I think we could be good together. Does he see that? Or is he too angry with me to realize it?

The sound of rustling fabric tells me Perry is shedding his shirt and I'm so tempted to watch. To lust over his chest and abs. But I refuse to look at him, afraid he might stop.

And that is the last thing I want.

The thump of shoes being kicked off sounds

next. The clank of his belt buckle. His accelerated breaths. The whir of a zipper being undone. I lie there among the rose petals, breathing heavily, my skin prickling with awareness. His eyes are on me. I can feel them.

Slowly I lift up my knees, keeping my head on the mattress, my ass up in the air. I stretch my arms out so they're above my head, crushing the petals, and I grip a few in my palms, turning my wrists so my hands are angled toward me, releasing the petals so they rain down upon me.

"Fuck," Perry groans and the triumph that races through my blood nearly has me laughing. With joy.

With victory.

He rests his hand on my right ass cheek, his fingers splayed, teasing the edge of my thong where it curves over the very top of my ass. I arch into his palm, seeking more but he doesn't give it to me.

"I suppose I can fuck you on our wedding night, right, wife?" He slips his fingers beneath the lacy strand that runs between my ass cheeks, tugging. The fabric tightens around my pussy, my now throbbing clit, and I close my eyes, wishing he'd do it again.

"Yes," I whisper and thank God he does it

again. Pulling on the lacy strip of fabric so it cuts against my delicate skin, making me hiss in pain. In pleasure.

His hands are on my hips, fingers curling around the lace as he slowly pulls them down, revealing everything. He stops when the fabric is around the tops of my thighs, binding me so I can't move before he slips two fingers inside of me without warning.

I cry out, bucking against his hand, and when he removes them, I whimper.

"Fucking soaked," he says, sounding pleased as he jams them back inside of me. "You actually like it when I'm mad at you?"

"No," I moan. I hate it when he's mad at me. I don't like it when anyone is angry with me, but there is something about fierce, arrogant Perry that is just...doing it for me.

He's the complete opposite of how he behaved last night. When he was sweet yet sexy and completely overcome by me. That had been thrilling. Exciting.

Tonight's version of my husband is even more so.

He continues fucking me with his fingers, slipping them in and out of my pussy at a steady pace. I start to move with him, straining towards my orgasm that's already on the horizon. I can almost reach it. I'm getting closer and closer…

Perry removes his fingers from my body completely and then his hand is coming around my throat, lifting me up before he shoves his fingers into my mouth.

"Suck," he demands and I do so, tasting myself as I lick my tongue around his fingers and suck with all my might.

What am I doing? What is he doing? He's suddenly cold and cruel and my body lights up like a Christmas tree, wanting more. Aching for him to fill me.

"Get up." His hand returns to my neck and he lightly tugs, until I'm on my knees with him pressed directly behind me. The heat of his skin sears into mine, though he's still wearing his boxers. His cotton-covered cock presses against my ass and a whimper escapes me when his fingers tighten around my throat, just enough to make my breath catch. "I'm so fucking pissed at you, Charlotte."

I swallow hard, about to say something but he places his other hand over my mouth, silencing me.

"Don't bother defending yourself. I know you want me to believe you had nothing to do with him showing up."

He rubs his fingers against my lips, mashing them, his index finger slipping into my mouth and touching my front teeth. I lick the tip of his finger and he growls into my ear. "Look at you, all the rose petals stuck to your skin."

I glance down at myself, realizing that he's right. I'm covered with them, though they're also falling off, one by one. He removes his hand from my neck, sliding it down, brushing away the petals. He cups one breast, then the other, pinching my nipples, his hold almost brutal and yet I whimper anyway.

He's not treating me like a delicate doll, and oh God, I like it.

His hand drifts across my trembling stomach, then lower. Teasing me before he reaches forward and scoops up a handful of rose petals off the bed.

And then promptly smashes them against my pussy.

Their silky softness contrasts with the rough way he's touching me and I tilt my head back, leaning against his shoulder as I moan into his fingers. He's still clutching my lower face, his other hand rubbing, crushing the petals into my sticky wet folds, and when he circles my clit, my entire body begins to shake.

Blindly I reach behind, my arm going around his nape as I slide my fingers into his soft hair. I cling to him, my hips moving as his fingers rub and circle, playing with my clit, driving me out of my mind. Until I'm coming, so hard I can barely breathe as the shivers consume me completely.

He whispers filthy things in my ear as I come. How fucking wet I am and how good I feel. Slick and hot. Asking me if I like it when he fucks me with his fingers. How he's going to fill me with his cock and make me come all over again.

This new, angry side to Perry is hot. Addicting. I can only whimper and moan, my skin coated with sweat from the intensity of my orgasm. I angle my head toward his and he kisses me, a savage taking of my mouth, his tongue thrusting, his fingers still pressed against my pussy.

"I own this," he whispers against my lips, his fingers clamping tighter, making me tremble. "You're mine now, wife. And if I have to fuck that asshole out of your thoughts over and over again until you don't even remember his name, then I will." His fingers slide inside of me, holding there. "Watch me."

CHAPTER EIGHT

Perry

ONCE CHARLOTTE HAS come down from her orgasm, and I've composed myself as much as possible, I flip her over on the bed so she's facing me. Her skin is flushed and damp, a few rose petals sticking here and there as she lies in the middle of them. The heart shape is long gone, the heady scent of the flowers filling my head. So strongly I swear I can taste it.

Can still taste her too. Salty and musky sweet.

I reach for her panties and tug them all the way off, my eyes narrowing when she slides her legs open, revealing herself completely to me. Pink and glistening and so damn pretty. I reach for her, trailing my fingers along the inside of her damp thigh, noting the way she shivers at my touch.

This isn't fake. My wife wants me, and that

fills me with a certain satisfaction that shouldn't feel so damn good, yet it does. Our situation is unusual. Fucking crazy if we're being real right now.

But in this moment, I wouldn't have it any other way. She understands where she fits into my life. Just like I know where I fit into hers.

I meant what I said, though. I will fuck that McTiernan asshole right out of her thoughts. Her memories. Her everything.

Like her heart.

He can't have it, especially if I can't either.

Running my hands down her smooth legs, I clamp my fingers around her ankles and spread her even wider. As wide as she can go. She watches me with a hint of fear in her eyes, though she must know I'd stop if she was truly scared.

Meaning I don't think she's afraid at all. She seems to like it. How rough I'm being. It's not my usual style, but damn. When I undressed her earlier, this foreign, possessive urge took over me, filling me with the need to show her who she belongs to.

Me.

I never want her to forget it.

I climb onto the mattress and rain kisses all over her thighs, her glistening pussy calling to me.

I lick at her clit. Swirl my tongue across it. Around it. Draw it between my lips and suck on it. Hard.

She lifts her hips, seeking more of my attention and I let go, moving away. Abandoning her completely so I can get rid of my boxer briefs and slip on a condom.

I'm fucking her. I told myself I wouldn't, but it's my right. My duty as her husband. It's our wedding night and this is expected. I'm fucking her and making her mine.

Charlotte rises up on her elbows, her gaze zeroed in on my hands. I grip the base of my cock and roll the condom on, her eyes flaring with heated anticipation. She's greedy for it.

Greedy for me.

"You want it?"

Her gaze finds mine, those blue eyes extra big as she nods.

"Say it." I get back onto the bed and she closes her legs, giving me room to climb on top of her, until my knees are on either side of her hips and our chests are pressed together, my face in hers. "Tell me you want it."

"I want you."

"Tell me exactly what you want."

"I want your—cock." Her cheeks turn pink

when she says the word, which is fucking adorable.

"Tell me you want me to fuck you."

She doesn't even hesitate. "I want you to fuck me."

I rise up, gripping the base of my dick and dragging the head through her soaked folds. "Say my name, baby."

"Perry." She closes her eyes when I nudge my cock against her clit.

"Open your eyes," I demand and they fly open. "I want you to know exactly who's fucking you tonight."

Her lips fall open as I ram myself inside, not being gentle about it at all. She can take me though. She's so damn wet and loose for me, but the fit is still snug. All that wet heat envelops my dick with a stranglehold, making me pause so I can take a few deep, controlling breaths.

Being inside of her feels like fucking heaven. If I let go now, I'll come too fast, and this time I'm prolonging it.

This time, I want to have a marathon fucking session with my wife.

I fuck her hard and steadily, spearing in and out of her welcoming body, the juicy sounds of her pussy filling the room. Her gaze stays on mine as I fuck her and I'm glad for it. She needs to know who she belongs to now.

And she can never forget it either.

She wraps those long legs around my hips, anchoring herself to me and I drop my head to her chest, fucking her in earnest. Our bodies stick together thanks to all the sweat, and the rose petals are still everywhere too.

An idea forms and I pull out of her completely. A protesting sound leaves her and I flip her over onto her stomach, pleased to see so many damn red rose petals yet again clinging to her skin.

"Get on your hands and knees," I command her and she does what I ask without protest, rising up and wagging that perfect petal-covered ass in my direction.

I slide into her from behind, filling her to the hilt, making her cry out. She goes completely still, adjusting to me buried inside of her, her hips shifting, sending me a little bit deeper.

Until I'm as deep as I can get.

"Oh God," she chokes out. "It feels—you feel so much fuller like this."

I start moving. In and out. Again and again. My gaze focused on the way my cock slides into her pussy, then out.

Fuck.

She's so damn noisy as I fuck her and my brain goes blank. The tingling at the base of my spine starts, settling into my balls, and I increase my pace, grunting with every thrust. Pumping in and out of her faster and faster until my entire body goes still and then the shudders start.

The shakes.

"Fuck. Charlotte." Her name falls from my lips the exact moment the orgasm slams into me, rendering me stupid. Her inner walls clench me tight, intensifying the already strong orgasm shaking throughout my body and I fall over her as it subsides, the both of us collapsing onto the bed, me curling around her.

Our ragged breathing is loud and I swear to fucking God my heart is going to pop out of my chest. She's shivering in my arms, my cock still embedded inside of her and she snuggles closer, her ass pressed right up against me.

My cock surges back to life, just like that.

I brush her ruined hair to the side, pressing my mouth against her nape. "Did you come?"

She nods. "A little one."

I feel as if my life has been completely transformed with one orgasm and she calls hers a little one.

Then I remember I already made her come once and then I don't feel so bad.

My hands roam upward, cupping and kneading her tits, my fingers curling around her stiffened nipples. The need to maul her is fucking strong, and I don't know where it's coming from. "We should do that again."

"I hope you brought more condoms."

"I brought an entire fucking box." Our overnight bags were delivered to the suite sometime during the wedding, thank Christ. I didn't have to think of one fucking thing the entire day. Sounds like much of the same is going to happen during our honeymoon.

I frown, thinking of it. Do I really want to be away in Mexico with my bride or would I rather be home doing a deep dive on a certain Morelli relative and figuring out ways to get him out of my wife's life permanently?

She reaches behind her, tugging pins out of her hair and tossing them onto the floor, making me chuckle. "You've ruined me."

"Good." I kiss her shoulder. "You needed to be ruined."

A sigh leaves her. "I should take a shower."

"I'll join you."

She's silent for a moment, contemplating

what I said, I'm sure. "How can you have sex with someone like that if you don't even trust them?"

I shrug. "You just make it so damn easy, Charlotte. Why shouldn't I fuck you? You're my wife now. It's your job to please me."

She goes quiet, and for a second, I regret saying that.

But damn it, it's the truth. I'm mad, but my anger doesn't dilute my attraction for her. In the moment, it only seemed to amplify my feelings. I wanted her.

I still want her.

Any way I can get her.

"You're right," she finally says, turning to look at me, those blue eyes of hers eating me up. "I guess I'm so starved for affection I'll take what I can get from you. Even if you hate me."

I say nothing. Just crawl out of bed and head for the bathroom, flicking on the lights to find the shower stall is massive, with two showerheads and a marble bench that's the perfect height for my bride to sit on and suck my cock while the hot spray of water drips down her smooth skin.

Perfect.

CHAPTER NINE

Charlotte

THE MOMENT WE exit the private plane Winston arranged to take us to Mexico, I breathe a sigh of relief.

The air is warm and smells of the sea. The wind whips my hair into complete disarray and I wish I would've put it in a ponytail.

But I can't complain. We're away from New York and Bishop's Landing. Away from our families and the threat of Seamus. The wedding and all the planning that came with it is finally over, and I'm glad.

So glad.

I know all of this is temporary, but I need the escape. I need to rest and relax and forget about my troubles at least for a little while. I know they'll all be waiting for me when we return home, but for now?

I want to banish them from my thoughts and enjoy my honeymoon. Even if my husband is acting standoffish this morning. Since we woke up, he hasn't said much. I blame it on him being tired. Yesterday was exhausting, both mentally and physically. Or maybe he's still wound up over Seamus showing up at the reception. I know if the tables were turned, I would be.

Somehow, I need to convince my husband that he can trust me. That's where a nice, relaxing, hopefully sex-filled honeymoon comes into play.

There's a car waiting for us that Perry's brother arranged and we're escorted to it immediately, the cool air-conditioning wrapping all around us as we settle onto the soft leather seats. We wait in the idling car as our luggage is loaded into the trunk and I cast a quick glance at my husband.

He's not paying attention to me in the least. Too busy tapping away on his phone, his brows lowered in seeming concentration. Or anger.

I can't really tell.

Deciding I can play this game, I pull my phone out of my bag to check if I have any messages. There's only one.

From my new sister-in-law.

Tinsley: *Hope you have fun in Mexico! Win-*

> *ston asked me to pick out clothes for your trip. I hope you like them.*

After the message is a string of winking-faced emojis, which tells me that the majority of the clothes she chose for me are probably sexy.

Before last night, I would've been nervous at the prospect. But now…

Now I know Perry is aroused by me. I may as well flaunt it if I've got it, right?

Yes. Right.

I send Tinsley a quick text.

> ***Me:*** *Thank you so much for doing that! I can't wait to see what you chose.*

I then send her a string of heart emojis.

It means so much to me, how kind she is. How open and accepting. I need that right now.

Desperately.

"Who are you texting?"

I glance up to find Perry watching me, his gaze wary despite the nonchalant tone. He's trying to play it cool, but I can tell he's suspicious.

"Your sister," I tell him, stashing my phone into my bag. "Tinsley."

He doesn't reply, but the relief on his face is evident and he averts his head, gazing out the window.

We don't say anything else during the car ride, and when we finally pull into the resort's driveway, I'm dying for actual conversation. Though I refuse to be the one who starts it.

Instead, I focus on the beautiful resort. The lush green lawn and the palm trees swaying with the breeze. The shimmering ocean just beyond the sprawling buildings. By the time we're climbing out of the car and entering the open-air lobby to check in, I'm gawking like a girl who's never traveled before, captivated by the nature that surrounds us. I'm such a city girl and I'm not used to this.

I wander the lobby while Perry takes care of matters at the front desk, spying a nearby restaurant featuring an outdoor patio with ocean views to die for. There's a giant pool in the near distance, the lounge chairs surrounding it filled with vacationers sunning themselves. I wonder if Tinsley packed me any swimsuits.

I'm sure she did. I'd guess they're all skimpy too.

"We have a private villa," Perry announces to me once he's finished checking in. "Winston went all out."

Excitement ripples down my spine but I keep a straight face. "That sounds—nice."

"I'm sure it is. Come on."

Once we arrive where we're staying, I'm taken aback at the extravagance. The villa is huge, with four bedrooms, three bathrooms, and a gorgeous kitchen I will never, ever touch. The living room is massive, with giant white couches covered in brightly printed pillows. There is vibrant art on the walls. Two of the bedrooms match in size with sumptuous linens on the bed, and both of them have an outdoor shower.

I'll be taking a shower outdoors!

I can't get over it.

Tile floors and cool air and crisp linens on the bed. Sunken couches and vibrant art on the walls. A big-screen TV I plan on never watching once.

We have our own private backyard and could probably fit two hundred people back here. There's a small infinity pool that's for our use and no one else's. There's also a path that leads from the backyard to the ocean and the resort's private beach.

It's like we've entered our own dream world.

"I'm going to take this bedroom," Perry tells me as he pauses in front of the open doorway. "You can have that one."

He nods toward the equally large bedroom across the hall from his.

My dreams come crashing down around me, just like that.

Standing taller, I clear my throat and make my approach, taking my new luggage with me. I don't bother protesting. "Okay."

I walk past him into my bedroom, settling the suitcase on the stand and zipping it open, curious to see what awaits me inside. I've never had anyone shop for me like this before, and as I dig through the clothing that lies within, I'm pleased to see I like all of it. Tinsley chose a variety of sundresses, T-shirts, and shorts. Tank tops. Panties and a couple of bras in the right size. So many two-piece swimsuits I could never wear them all. They are colorful and just as I predicted—skimpy.

There's a toiletries bag full of the essentials, mostly items I've used before or always wanted to try. There's another small bag full of brand-new cosmetics. There's a curling iron and a brush and comb and shampoo and conditioner. She thought of everything.

There's also a note from Tinsley, written in swirling script.

I hope I covered all of the bases and you have everything you need. When my brother told me what he wanted to do for you guys, I said it was impossible. Yet here I am, making it possible for him. Really for you. I hope you have a wonderful time with Perry. Happy honeymoon!

Love, your new sister,
Tins

I sniff, blinking away the tears as I finish her note. She's so thoughtful. I've never had a sister before. I like the idea of Tinsley and I becoming closer.

I need as many allies as I can get in the Constantine family.

Giddy with excitement I choose one of the bikinis from the many Tinsley provided for me and dart off into the bathroom, shedding my clothes and leaving them on the floor before I put on the hot-pink string bikini that fits perfectly.

Thank God I had that wax treatment at the spa before the wedding. I wouldn't have been able to get away with wearing this prior to that spa visit.

After I pull my hair into a high ponytail, I check myself out in the mirror, wondering what Perry will think of this bikini. And me.

Does he even think about me? Last night more than proved that—maybe. Well, it proved that he's definitely attracted to me. But since we woke up this morning, he's been indifferent. As if I don't really matter.

That hurts.

Lifting my chin, I reach for the small bottle of lotion the hotel provides and lather it on, making sure every bit of skin exposed is silky smooth. Meaning I went completely through one of those tiny bottles. The tropical scent lingers in the air, and I smile at my reflection before I flee the bathroom.

Only to run directly into my husband, who for some reason is in my bedroom.

Shirtless.

Only wearing a pair of black and gray swim trunks.

Looking far too delicious to ignore.

"Sorry." He grabs hold of my arms to steady me, keeping me close. "Didn't mean to run into you."

"What are you doing in here?" I hate how breathless I sound and I clear my throat, forcing myself to act as nonchalant as possible.

Like it's no big deal that my sexy husband is pressed against me and we're on a honeymoon that is supposedly in name only.

Please. All I can think about is the next time I

can get him naked again.

"I came looking for you," he says, his voice low as he takes a single step away from me, still holding on to my arms. "I'm going out to the pool. Wanted to ask if you'd join me."

I refuse to let what he said fill me with hope. His seeking me out means nothing. "I had the same idea."

His gaze lingers on all the exposed bits of me—which are a lot. "I see that."

"Is there any sunscreen around?" I ask, meeting his gaze.

"Probably." He releases me and heads out of the bedroom. "Let's go look."

I follow after him, taking in the tattoo that's in the center of his back. A sprawling oak tree with intricate branches and a strong, solid trunk. The question slips from my lips before I can stop it.

"What's the tattoo represent?"

He glances over his shoulder at me. "Family."

That's all he says, but it's enough. I've come to realize family is very important to him. He loves his mother and younger sister. Respects and admires his oldest brother. He even has a tattoo that represents him and his brothers with the three swords. He's a loyal man, and not just because of his tattoos. Those are meaningless without actions.

His actions tell me he loves his family very much, and I take comfort in that. He's not a bad person. He cares. He loves. Freely.

What would it be like, to be loved by Perry Constantine? To know that he's loyal to you no matter what.

If I'm lucky, maybe I'll know someday.

"Here's the sunscreen."

I realize I've followed Perry into the kitchen and he's found a couple of cans of spray sunscreen on the kitchen counter, close to the sliding glass door that leads out to the pool. He grabs one and heads outside and I go with him, shutting the sliding glass door before I turn to face him.

"Want me to spray you?" he pops the lid off the sunscreen and aims it right at me.

"I can do it myself."

"Thought I'd offer." He shrugs and hands it over, which I apply liberally everywhere I can reach, except my back.

Can't really reach that.

"Here." He takes the can from me. "Turn around."

I do as he says, shivering when the cold spray hits my skin. He coats my shoulders and back.

My lower back, just above my butt. My thighs and calves. Even my ass cheeks.

"Don't want you to get burned." He steps closer, stopping directly behind me before he hands me the can. "Will you spray me?"

I grab the sunscreen and turn to face him, frowning. "You can't do it yourself?"

"I'd rather you did it." He smiles. "Please?"

How can I resist?

I spray him everywhere, marveling at how handsome he is when he tips his head back and closes his eyes, holding his arms straight out. He's muscular yet lean. Broad but not too bulky. Covered in tats with six-pack abs and trim hips. Muscular thighs and legs that are covered in light brown hair, but not *too* covered.

Everything about my husband is just right.

"Turn around," I tell him and he does so without complaint, hanging his head as I spray his shoulders and back. Dip down to spray the back of his legs. By the time I'm finished, there's a light cloud of sunscreen surrounding us and I'm coughing, which makes him chuckle.

My heart leaps at the sound and I tell myself to stop it.

I set the can onto a nearby glass table before I return my attention to Perry. "You're done."

He turns to face me once more. "You hungry?"

I shrug. My appetite has shrunk lately, thanks to the stress of our wedding.

"We can call for room service if you want. They'll bring us drinks and poolside snacks," Perry says.

"What kind of poolside snacks?" My stomach growls as it's wont to do when I talk about food.

"Whatever you want. Chips and salsa. Guacamole. A cheeseburger. I was looking at the menu a few minutes ago. They've got a lot."

"I'll think about it." I wander over to one of the lounge chairs and drop onto the plush cushion, arranging myself just so before I slip on the large sunglasses that I always keep in my bag. I can feel Perry's gaze on me and I close my eyes, wondering what he's thinking.

Then I hear a loud splash, water droplets hitting my skin and making me squeal. When I open my eyes, I find Perry treading water in the middle of the pool, watching me carefully.

"Aren't you going to swim?"

"I wanted to get some sun first."

"You put on sunscreen."

"I'll still get some color on my skin if I sit out here. This sun is pretty intense," I tell him, vaguely annoyed.

"I thought you'd swim with me." His expression is pure hurt little boy, which doesn't go along at all with the rough man who fucked me last night.

Is he for real right now?

"I didn't think you'd want to do anything with me," I retort.

He tilts his head to the side, ignoring my comment. "Where'd you get that bikini anyway? Tinsley?"

I nod, lifting my knees so my feet are propped on the cushion.

"I like it."

That's all he says before he dives underneath the water but it's enough to make my skin buzz and my heart trip over itself.

He likes it.

But will he ever like me?

CHAPTER TEN

Perry

I SWAM. I ate. I sat out on one of those loungers like Charlotte and fell asleep. Only to wake up almost two hours later to the setting sun and scorched skin.

Charlotte only laughed at me. I think she likes to see me in pain.

Guess I can't blame her, with the way I treated her this morning on the plane over here. I was in a mood. Sullen. Grumpy. Tempted to text Winston and ask him if he's found anything out about Seamus McFuckface yet, but I restrained myself.

The guy doesn't work that fast and it's a Sunday. Winston probably won't launch into his investigation until first thing Monday morning, which is fine. I need to chill.

But damn it, I want to know what's up with

that guy. Why did he show up at my reception? Does he actually want Charlotte?

Tough shit, he can't have her.

Memories of last night pop into my brain as I take a cool shower and I revel in them for a moment. The sounds Charlotte made when I fucked her with my fingers. How responsive she is, even when I'm mean. And I'm never mean.

I used to be the good time guy. Both in person and privately. I'm easygoing, even in bed. Especially in bed.

First night with Charlotte and I lose all control. Second night? I act like a complete macho dick, and wouldn't you know, my little wifey gets off on it.

Who fucking knew?

I made a reservation at one of the restaurants in the resort and I take my time getting ready since we're still an hour away from having to show up. I think about shaving but worry what that razor will feel like on my sunburned skin, so I take a pass. Instead, I try to get my hair to cooperate before I slip on a pair of black trousers and a white dress shirt. My usual outfit of choice. I put on a silver chain around my neck and a bunch of rings, not giving a fuck what anyone might think about me. Not even Charlotte.

She never said she minded the rings. And I'm wearing my wedding ring too, so that should please her, right?

By the time I'm leaving my bedroom in search of her, I'm jumpy. Anxious. Starving. I need food and alcohol, stat.

I find Charlotte sitting outside on her phone, the gentle breeze causing her hair to fly across her face. She keeps batting it away, her gaze on her screen, never noticing that I came outside and now I feel like a stalker.

But damn, she's pretty in the strapless black dress she's wearing, her pinkish golden sunburn on complete display. She's got a thin gold necklace around her neck and thin gold hoops in her ears, my ring twinkling on her left ring finger. Her nose is red from the sun and her lips are painted a pretty coral color. She glances up at the same time I shove my hands into my pockets and she does a double take when she sees me standing there.

"I didn't hear you come outside." She sets her phone on the table in front of her.

"Everything all right?" I flick my chin at her phone, the screen going black before I can catch what she was doing on it.

Charlotte's brows draw together. "Yes."

"Who were you texting?" I sound like a jealous prick, but I can't help it. I don't want her texting anyone. Not a single soul.

Especially not that dickbag.

"I was scrolling Instagram. I looked up the hashtag for this resort and was checking out the photos." Her smile is faint, and I refuse to react to it.

"You almost ready?" I ask, my voice rough.

She nods and checks her phone yet again. "We still have twenty minutes."

"They might seat us early. Plus, I'm starving." I flick my head. "Let's go. We can always sit in the bar and wait for our table. Have a drink."

"I'm not twenty-one yet," she reminds me, her voice soft.

I keep forgetting she's younger than me. She doesn't act like it. Well, sometimes she does.

Never in bed though.

"No one will card you," I reassure her. "And I'll order drinks for us."

"Okay." She pushes her chair back and rises to her feet before she makes her way over to me. I realize she's not wearing a dress at all but a strapless black jumpsuit thing that's all one piece.

And she looks hot as hell.

I run a hand over my mouth to smother

whatever I was about to say to her, unable to tear my gaze away from her chest. The top clings to her tits perfectly, giving me a nice view of her cleavage. The sides and back of her jumpsuit has cutouts, exposing even more skin and I'm fairly certain my wife isn't wearing a bra.

Fuck me.

"You ready to go, then?" she asks once she stops directly in front of me.

"Yeah. Let's do it."

"Let me grab my purse." She enters the house while I remain outside, my gaze locked on her, watching until she disappears into the bedroom.

I shake my head, scrubbing my hand over my face. Across the back of my neck.

This woman is going to completely undo me before this little honeymoon is through.

I know it.

✧ ✧ ✧

THE RESTAURANT IS open air and has a spectacular view of the ocean, which is now mostly shrouded in darkness thanks to the late hour. We ended up sitting in the bar for only twenty minutes before we were shown to our table and I notice the longer Charlotte sips on that giant pina colada she was desperate to order, the more relaxed she becomes.

"I love it here," she announces once she's slurped the last of her drink.

"Have you been to Mexico before?" I dunk a tortilla chip into a bowl of guac before I shove it into my mouth.

She shakes her head. "I've been to the Caribbean. Hawaii. But never Mexico."

"I'm surprised. Figured you Lancasters travel all over the world."

"Oh we do. Or we used to, when I was much younger. All Lancasters go to Lancaster Prep, so we end up spending most of our time there during high school," she explains.

I've heard of Lancaster Prep. A very expensive, elite boarding school where the children of the best of the best—and the richest of the rich—attend. "All your brothers went there?"

"Yes, and Crew's there now. He's a senior. All of my cousins attended or are attending. It's a Lancaster family tradition."

"Your family has lots of traditions?"

"Oh definitely. Many of them are downright archaic." She smiles faintly. "Like this arranged marriage thing."

I can't help the chuckle that slips out. "My mother tried to get every single one of my brothers and sisters to marry someone of her choosing."

"Every single one?"

I nod.

"And did she succeed?"

I slowly shake my head. "Only with me so far."

We're both quiet for a moment, letting that sink in.

"Can I admit something to you?" she asks me once the server drops her off a fresh pina colada.

I watch as she takes a generous sip. "Go for it."

"I was jealous of Ash." She leans back in her chair while I absorb what she just said.

"Why?"

"I thought she was too—clingy towards you."

I gape at her. "What?"

"She hung all over you the night of our engagement party." A scowl forms on her face. "I didn't like it."

Wait a minute.

"Charlotte, are you telling me you were jealous of her because of me?"

"I wasn't jealous of her relationship with Winston if that's what you were originally thinking." She takes another sip from her drink and my gaze settles on her pursed lips. "I thought maybe there was something going on between you two."

I want to laugh, but I don't. When I first met Ash, I thought she was hot. And she was on my side. I liked that. But I'm not attracted to her. She belongs to Winston. He'd have my ass if I even looked at Ash wrong.

Besides, he's my brother and I would never do him dirty like that.

"There's nothing going on between me and Ash," I say, my voice quiet. "There never has been. She's with Winston. She's his wife."

"I know." She nods. Sighs. "I'm silly. I just—she's beautiful."

"She is," I agree.

Pain flickers in Charlotte's eyes. "And sophisticated. She fits into the Constantine family perfectly."

I bark out a laugh. "It wasn't always like that. Trust me. My mother hated her."

"Really?" She sounds surprised.

"Definitely." My gaze tracks her every little movement. How she tucks a wild strand of blonde hair behind her ear. How there's another strand stuck to her upper lip thanks to the gloss she's wearing. She tugs the stray hair away, her index finger lingering at the corner of her mouth and heat surges inside of me.

I'm filled with the sudden urge to kiss her.

"Does your mother hate me?" she asks.

I slowly shake my head when her gaze finds mine. "Sometimes I think she likes you better than me."

She laughs. "I doubt that. She dotes on you. I think you're her favorite."

"Only because I kiss her ass," I mutter.

"No. It's more than that, and you don't have to act like a tough guy in front of me like you do everyone else. It's okay to admit you love your mother and that you're close to her." Her smile is small, her eyes full of sadness. "I'm not close to either of my parents. They don't seem to care much for me."

My heart breaks for this girl. Woman.

My wife.

"Who are you close to in your family? Any of them?"

"Mainly Crew. We're close in age and our brothers are a lot older than us, so we spent most of our growing-up years together. My mother tries, but I'm not like her at all. I don't want to shop or gossip, and those are her two favorite things to do." She looks away, her lips parted, her expression thoughtful. "As we got older, Crew and I grew more distant. He's a Lancaster male, after all. He can't be too soft and spend so much time with his sister."

The Lancasters are the worst, I swear to God.

"It's why Seamus knew he could take advantage of me," she continues.

Shock courses through me at hearing his name—mixed with a fair amount of anger. "How did he take advantage of you?"

Her gaze finds mine, those blue eyes full of unfamiliar emotion. "I don't want to talk about it on our honeymoon, but...you have to believe me, Perry. I didn't want him at our wedding. There's no way I would've wanted him near me, after what he's done. And I didn't invite him either. Isn't it your family who's big on keeping their archrivals close at hand?"

Winston told me exactly that. He even said McLoser could show up. I don't know why I'm so focused on the fact that Charlotte invited that asshole.

Our server arrives with our meals, interrupting our conversation, and we eat in comfortable silence, commenting on how delicious the food is. How I think Charlotte should slow down on the pina coladas, but she ignores me and orders another one, hiccupping in the middle of her request, which makes her laugh.

My wife is well on her way to being drunk.

I think about what she said, the earnestness in her gaze, and I realize…

I believe her. She didn't invite him.

Still think she's keeping plenty of secrets though.

"I like your rings," she tells me after we're done eating. She's still working on her drink and I'm long done with mine.

I glance down at my hands. "You do?"

Nodding, she extends her hand. "Can I look at them?"

I offer her my right hand first and she holds it between her own and bends her head, her mouth so close she could kiss my still slightly battered knuckles. She pulls away slightly to really examine the rings, running a finger over one. Then another.

I shouldn't like it when she touches me, but I do. I don't want her to worm her way into my heart. I still don't one hundred percent trust her or her intentions. That Seamus guy showing up ruined everything, but it also taught me a lesson. One I shouldn't forget.

Never let my guard down. I did that with Charlotte way too soon and look at me now.

Making an ass out of myself at my own damn wedding reception by socking my new wife's ex-lover in the face. I'm shocked as hell I haven't heard from Mom yet, or from Charlotte's parents.

I'm sure their response is coming.

"Let me see your other hand," Charlotte demands, pulling me from my thoughts.

I offer her my left hand and she immediately traces the band around my ring finger. It's platinum. Simple. No stones or design. Exactly what I would've wanted in a wedding ring, not that she ever consulted me before she got it.

Where she got it, I have no idea. It was brand new, nary a scratch on it. I believed wearing it would feel like a shackle around my neck, but so far, so good.

"Do you like your wedding ring?" she asks, her gaze meeting mine across the table, my hand still clutched in between both of hers.

"Yeah. It goes well with the rest of my collection," I say almost flippantly.

Her smile is slow. Sexy as fuck. "That's why I chose it."

"You picked it out?"

"Of course." She lets go of my hand and leans back in her chair, indignant. "Did you choose my wedding ring?"

"Maybe." I decide to fuck with her.

She scowls, taking the bait. "Maybe?"

I shrug a shoulder. "I was getting busier and busier at work right before the wedding. I didn't have a lot of time."

The hurt is back, lingering in her eyes, and I immediately feel like a jackass. "Your mother chose it, then?"

A ragged sigh leaves me and I scrub a hand across my chin, wincing thanks to my sunburn. "You want the truth?"

She nods.

"I went with her and picked it out."

Her smile is back. She looks very pleased with herself. "Good."

For someone who originally protested this entire marriage scenario, she now seems totally into it. "You like it?"

Her gaze drops to her left hand. "I love it."

"I'm glad." The server drops off the check and I add a generous tip before I add the meal to our room. "Ready to get out of here?"

She nods, rising to her feet. "Let's go."

I follow her as we exit the restaurant, noting the appreciative glances she receives from male diners. I glare at every one of them, making it clear that I don't approve and she doesn't even realize what's going on.

How much she affects me.

How possessive she makes me feel.

How I can't wait to get back to our private villa so I can fuck her on the couch.

Or the kitchen counter.

Maybe we could go outside and I can fuck her on a lounge chair.

I'm up for any of it.

All of it.

Chapter Eleven

Charlotte

I WAKE UP slowly, my head throbbing in time with my heartbeat. I try to open my eyes but my lids feel as if they're weighed down with concrete blocks and it pains me to make the attempt.

So I remain lying there, the fan on above me cooling my heated skin.

I don't remember actually going to bed. Or falling asleep. The last thing I recall is entering the villa with Perry. I threw myself at him, almost stumbling and he grabbed hold of me, his touch firm as he murmured, "You're drunk, wife."

I frown, then immediately try to relax my forehead. Even that hurts.

Oh God, I think I'm hungover.

There's a soft knock coming from somewhere and then I hear the door open. Almost immediately I can smell my husband, his cologne mixed with his distinct, delicious scent, yet I don't move. It's like I can't.

"You're awake?" He's whispering, which is such a relief.

"Yes," I croak, my throat dry. Like I swallowed ten cotton balls and they're all clogged in my throat.

"I brought you something to drink." He speaks in what I assume is a normal tone as he enters the room and I roll over on my side, clamping my hand over my exposed ear.

"Please stop yelling," I request weakly.

He chuckles and I hear the thunk of heavy glass being set onto the nightstand. "I'm not."

I crack a single eye open but I don't see him anywhere. "What did you bring me?"

"A glass of water and a bottle of ibuprofen." I hear the snap of a lid and the rattle of pills. Even that sounds too loud. "You should take four."

"I don't know if I can swallow them down," I admit.

"Charlotte." He lowers his voice. "Sit up."

I do as he says, keeping my eyes tightly closed. My head swims, and I'm afraid if I see what's actually going on, I might throw up.

"Open your eyes."

Slowly I crack open my lids, wincing for a moment before I realize there's no glare in the room. No bright sunlight or lamp on. It's dim and quiet and the fan is whirring overhead.

"Look at me."

I do as he says, slowly turning my head in the direction of his voice until there he is, standing beside my bed looking as casual as I think I've ever seen him in a T-shirt and pair of shorts, his hair mussed, his skin not as red as it was last night.

Ugh. Last night…

"Hold your hand out," he tells me and I do as he says, watching as he dumps four ibuprofen into my palm. "Take a drink of water first."

Like a child being told what to do, I glance over at the nightstand and grab the glass of water, drinking half of it in big gulps. The water is cool and soothing on my dry throat and I drop the pills onto my tongue before I swallow them down.

"Finish the water," he says and I do so, draining every last drop until I set the glass in his offered hand.

I glance down at myself, frowning. "I'm wearing the same clothes from last night."

"Do you even remember last night?"

"We went to dinner."

"Yeah."

"I drank three pina coladas."

"Four," he corrects.

"Okay. Four. We left the restaurant." I frown, thinking. It hurts. "Came back here. I think I tripped?"

"I caught you."

"Uh-huh. And I was laughing." A lot. Too much.

"You wouldn't stop. Then you kept asking me the same question over and over. That's when I knew you were plastered. I eventually walked you into your bedroom and you collapsed on the bed. You fell asleep within minutes, and you were snoring." He smiles and lifts the empty glass up as if in a toast. "I'll get you more water."

Humiliation burns at his words and I shove it aside, telling myself it's fine.

I'm fine.

I watch him leave before I look down at myself again, my hair falling forward. I brush it out of my eyes and glance toward the dresser. The giant mirror that hangs above it. My reflection in said mirror.

I stare at my face in horror, a whimper escaping me.

Oh God. I look terrible.

My hair is a disaster, the elastic band dangling around a few strands in the weakest ponytail ever. There is so much makeup under my eyes I look like a raccoon. My eyes are bloodshot and my skin is blotchy and I swear to God my boobs are about to slip out of the top of this jumpsuit thing I'm wearing.

And I'm suddenly consumed with the need to pee.

I hop out of bed and rush into the bathroom, slamming the door so hard I wince. After I take care of business, I grab a clean washcloth and run it under the water in the sink before I scrub at my face, removing all of the eyeliner and mascara that settled beneath my eyes. I grab a brush and smooth out my hair as best as I can. Tug the top of my jumpsuit up so my chest is fully covered.

Okay. Now I'm a little more presentable.

Still got the headache though.

Taking a deep breath, I open the door and walk back into the bedroom the same time Perry reenters the room, a full glass of water clutched in his hand. He gives it to me and I murmur thank you before I take a few sips and set it on top of the dresser.

"You look better," he says, his gaze scanning me up and down.

"I should shower." The second the words leave me, I remember the shower we took together on our wedding night. How I sat on that marble bench and gave him a blow job until he couldn't take it anymore. He ended up holding me against the wall while he fucked me until we were both coming, our moans echoing in the bathroom.

The moment was hot. Seared into my memory forever.

"Finish your water first." His deep voice pulls me from my thoughts.

I take another sip like the docile wife I am. "I have a question."

"What is it?"

"What did I keep asking you last night?" I'm curious.

He smiles. "You sure you want to hear it?"

I nod, fighting the unease. "Definitely."

"You wanted to know." He takes a step closer, drawing his fingers across the top of the dresser. "If I thought." He stops directly in front of me, his body heat ratcheting up my temperature level. "You were sexy."

My mouth drops open. "I did not."

"Yes, you did."

I sort of want to die. Why do I always turn

into a fool for him? Why am I so damn insecure? I blame my parental issues for that one. Clearly I wasn't held enough as a child. "That's kind of pathetic."

"I thought it was cute." He bops the tip of my nose with his index finger. "Take a shower and let's go to brunch."

"What time is it?"

"Nine thirty."

I'm gaping at him again. "It's that early? Really? Why didn't you let me sleep in?"

"I got bored." He shrugs before he heads out of my bedroom. "Hurry up. I'm starving."

I turn and watch him go, stumped when he shuts the door behind him. Like, what just happened? Why was he being so sweet and taking care of me? The man is a contradiction, though I'm sure he could feel the same way about me. I send him mixed messages on a daily basis.

Looks like he does the same to me.

I take a shower and wash my hair. Slip on a white string bikini and pull a delicate flower-print dress on over it. I pull my damp hair into a bun on top of my head and slip on the hoops I wore last night, then apply a little bit of mascara on my lashes and slick a rosy-pink lip balm on my lips.

There. I'm done.

I slip on a pair of leather slide sandals and walk out into the living room to find it empty. As is the kitchen.

As is the rest of the house.

It's only when I return to the living room do I hear a splash from outside and realize Perry is in the pool.

Heading outside, I stop at the edge of the pool and watch him swim across the length of it. He pops his head out of the water and slicks his hair back with his hands, his gaze finding mine.

"I got bored again," he says in answer to my unspoken question.

I can only shake my head.

"And I ordered room service instead. It should be here any second."

"I got dressed up for nothing." I wave a hand at my outfit.

"I think you look nice." His smile is vaguely naughty.

That look in his eyes dark.

"Gee thanks." I kick off my slides. Reach for the hem of my dress before I whip it off and over my head, letting it fall onto the lounger I'm standing next to. I stand there for just a moment, letting Perry get a good, long look at me in this bikini that's made of scraps before I'm diving into the water and swimming toward him.

Until my head is out of the water and I'm treading in front of him, breathing a little heavily as droplets coast down my face, dripping from my chin.

"Nice swimsuit."

He can't even see it at the moment. "It's not a swimsuit."

"What is it, then?"

"A bikini," I correct him.

"Not made of much."

I glance down to see my nipples poking against the thin white fabric. Maybe he can see more than I realized.

I return my gaze to his. "I know."

He reaches out and drifts his thumb against the very nipple I was just looking at. "Water too cold?"

"It's perfect."

He shifts closer, the water swirling around us. I scoot backward, until I'm against the wall of the pool, my back pressed to the slick tile, my feet firmly touching the bottom. Perry is standing in front of me, above me, water running down his bare chest, little paths snaking across his skin.

I want to lick the water. Lap at his skin with my tongue. Hear him hiss in a breath.

Without a word he rests his hand on my hip, his fingertips slipping just beneath the string of my bikini bottoms. Despite the cool water, I can feel the heat of his touch, branding my skin. Making my breaths come faster.

I'm trembling.

My eyes fall shut when he shifts even closer, his body pressed to mine, his heat seeping into me. He drifts his fingers down the front of my chest, in between my breasts, so lightly I could almost believe he's not touching me at all.

"I should hate you," he murmurs, his casually cruel words lashing at my heart.

"Why?" I croak, hating how sad I sound.

I don't want him to hate me—and I don't want to hate him either. We're stuck together. We should be allies, not enemies.

Here we go again with the mixed messages.

"I still don't trust you. Your ex showing up at our reception? That was fucked up." He slips his fingers into the front of my bikini top, sliding them up and down along my breast. "Winston believes you had something to do with him being there."

I open my eyes. "I already told you I didn't ask Seamus to come to our re—"

Perry clamps his hand over my mouth, silencing me. "Don't say his name."

I stare up at him, fear making my heart pound faster.

"I never want to hear you say his fucking name again, do you hear me?" When I nod, he slowly removes his hand. "My brother has launched a full investigation into that asshole."

"How do you know?"

"I spoke to him earlier on the phone." He glares at me. "You think I was just going to ignore what happened at our wedding? I'm not about to get played."

Plotting my demise without my knowledge during our honeymoon. How wonderful.

"I'm not trying to play you." Whatever that means. "And I don't understand the need to investigate…him."

What am I saying? I know Seamus didn't show up out of the blue just to say hi. He wants to cause trouble.

But why?

Perry blows out an aggravated breath. "Because he's related to the Morellis." His fingers find my nipple and he pulls and tugs, making me hiss in pain, yet he doesn't let up. "Morellis like to fuck with Constantines."

"I have nothing to do with this."

"You have everything to do with this." He grips my hip tightly, his voice fierce. "Don't act all innocent with me, Charlotte. Like you don't know how the real world works. You're not some sheltered little girl who was kept under lock and key all your life. You ran away to Paris and fucked your professor. There's nothing innocent about that."

Anger fills me and I try to jerk out of his hold but he won't let me go.

"Truth hurts, right? Think of how I felt when I saw that asshole lurking behind me at my own wedding reception," Perry tosses at me.

"You don't even care!" I try to shove at him but it's like attempting to move a steel wall. Impossible. "You don't care about me, or the stupid wedding, or the fact that I'm your wife. Stop trying to act all casual and happy-go-lucky on our supposed honeymoon. You're merely tolerating me so you can use me for sex."

"You like it though." His voice is calm. Cold. "You like it when I fuck you. Don't bother denying it."

Oh God, I wish I could.

"Let's test how much you hate it. Hate me." His hand dives into the front of my bikini bottoms, his fingers searching me. I'm wet, and it's not just from the damn pool. "Yep. You hate my guts."

His sarcastic tone makes me growl and I lunge for him, curling my hands around the back of his neck and tugging as hard as I can on his hair, trying to cause him pain. Anything to get him to stop touching me. Saying such rude things to me. "Let. Me. Go!"

"No." He shoves two fingers inside of me, making me moan like the weak woman that I am. In agony. In defeat. "Oh yeah. You really can't stand me now."

My hands fall to his shoulders and I cling to him, closing my eyes so I don't have to see the smug expression on his stupidly handsome face. I don't even know why we're arguing, but of course it leads to this.

It always leads to this.

A gasp escapes me when he removes his fingers from within my body and grabs hold of my waist, lifting me up. My legs automatically wrap around his hips, anchoring myself to him.

"Look at me," he demands and I slowly open my eyes to find his face in mine, his expression completely closed off, yet his eyes are full of turbulent emotion. "Don't ever forget who you belong to. You're a Constantine now."

I say nothing. There's no point in arguing because it's true. I am a Constantine now.

Whether I like it or not.

"If I ever find out that piece of shit tried to talk to you, I'm killing him." He leans in, his mouth at my temple, kissing me tenderly. "I don't care if it starts a full-scale war, I'll tear him apart, and enjoy every second of it too."

I'm trembling so hard my teeth start to chatter.

"Did you see they're talking about our wedding on the gossip sites?" His voice is so casual, yet also edged with fury.

"N-no." I shake my head.

"Tinsley sent me a few links earlier. She wanted to warn me." He tilts his head, his mouth brushing against mine as he speaks. "Not that I care. He's the asshole who shouldn't have been there, sniffing around his ex."

"I—"

He rests his fingers against my lips, silencing me. "Don't tell me how you feel about him, or me or anyone else. I don't want to know."

We stare at each other, our chests brushing with every accelerated breath, my core throbbing, my entire body aching.

Despite everything he just said, the threats he

made, and how scared I feel, there is one thing that still remains clear.

I want him. And he knows it.

I think he wants me too.

He pushes his fingers in between my lips and I let him, our gazes never straying. I pull them in further, licking his fingertips with my tongue and his eyelids grow heavy as he watches me suck his fingers like they're his dick.

"Did you ever suck his cock?" he asks me.

I pause, not wanting to answer him. He doesn't want to hear the truth.

But my pause is answer enough because he rips his fingers from my lips and kisses me, his mouth rough, his tongue like a weapon as it lashes with mine. I moan low in my throat, letting him do whatever he wants to me, knowing in the end I'll get what I want.

Him. Buried deep inside of me.

His hands are everywhere, tugging at my bikini, reaching behind me to undo the tie before he's shoving the top out of the way. He squeezes my breast, his fingers working my nipple as he continues to kiss me and I lean into his palm, craving more.

When he ends the kiss, I whimper, but he ignores me, wrapping his lips around my nipple.

A soft *oh* leaves me and I grip the back of his head, my fingers entwined with his wet hair as I hold him to me.

He sucks hard, his tongue lashing at my flesh before he pulls away, teasing my nipple with soft flickers of his tongue.

"This is what I wanted to do to you last night," he growls against my chest. "You were so fucking drunk, there was no way I was going to touch you."

"I wouldn't have stopped you," I admit.

He pauses, his gaze finding mine. "I wanted you to remember."

Perry continues lavishing his attention on my breasts. Until my bikini top is long gone, floating away on the water. I grip him to me, squeezing my legs around his hips, the unmistakable ridge of his erection pressed against my center and I shift my hips in an attempt to rub against him.

I slide my hand in between us, my fingers finding the front of his swim trunks and the tie at the center. With fumbling fingers, I undo it, until the trunks loosen around his waist and I'm sliding my hand down the front of him, finding his hard cock. I wrap my fingers around his shaft, squeezing him firmly and he pulls away from my chest. He thrusts his face in mine as he shoves his hand into my hair, holding me in place, his cock throbbing against my palm.

"Know what to do with it?" He thrusts his hips forward, surging into my grip.

"I think I can figure it out." I begin to stroke him. Up and down, nice and slow, my thumb circling around the tip over and over.

Without warning he finds my mouth, kissing me. Devouring me. All the while he nudges aside my bikini bottoms, bats my hand away from his dick and shoves his way inside of me before going completely still. Holding me to him for a long, quiet moment. The only thing I can focus on is his throbbing cock buried deep inside of my body.

Despite everything. The cruelty and the threats and the hatred and frustration, this is the confirmation I needed. He still wants me.

And I want him too.

"Perry." His name falls from my lips in a heated whisper and he swallows it, his tongue thrusting in time with the rhythm of his cock. He fucks me soundly in the pool, completely out of control, his movements sloppy and frantic, and oh God, it feels so good.

Too good.

It all happens so fast. The water is splashing around us because of our shifting bodies, and I'm moaning. Clutching him close. Squeezing my inner walls until it feels like I've got him locked deep.

He curses, pulling away from my lips to press his face against my shoulder. I wrap my arms around him, circling my hips, seeing stars when he hits a certain spot. He hits it again.

And again.

Until I'm clutched up and coming, panting in his ear, tugging on his hair as wave after wave slams into me. He's breathing hard, his entire body gone stiff just before an agonized groan leave him, a clue that he just came.

The other clue being when I feel him spill inside of me.

Without a condom.

Oh no.

I shove him away from me with all the strength I can muster, glaring at him in dismay, my breathing harsh, my heart racing. He watches me, diving his hand beneath the water I'm sure to cradle his precious, just-came-inside-of-me cock.

"I felt you come." My tone is accusatory.

He frowns, looking confused.

"You didn't use a condom."

"Aw, fuck." He grips the back of his neck with both hands before he smacks the water with them. "*Fuck.*"

I'm throbbing between my legs, my pussy extra sensitive and my clit feels as if it's on fire. Like I could come all over again if I just brushed my fingers against it.

The doorbell rings, indicating room service is here.

We stare at each other from across the water, the both of us still breathing heavily, the water dripping across Perry's handsome, angry face.

"I fucked up," he mutters as he climbs out of the water completely naked. "I'm sorry."

I watch him go, my gaze on his nude body. How comfortable he is in front of me without a stitch of clothing on.

"Are you going to answer the door like that?" I ask incredulously.

"Yes," he snaps, grabbing a towel from a nearby lounger and wrapping it around his waist before he heads inside the house to answer the door.

I duck under the water and swim beneath the surface, like I'm modest and don't want him to see me. Normally I would feel that way.

But he's seen everything, touched everything. Fucked me extra hard and came inside of me in the most careless way possible. I don't want babies with him. Not now.

Maybe not even ever.

CHAPTER TWELVE

Perry

WE EAT OUR breakfast quietly at the massive dining table, me sitting at the head while Charlotte sits to my right. I'm shoveling it in as fast as I can, like I can't get enough while she merely picks at her food. Swirling it around her plate with her fork, a sad expression on her pretty face.

She's wearing a hotel robe that completely engulfs her and I still have my towel on, naked beneath it. No reason to get dressed up for this meal, am I right?

I still can't believe how angry I got. How I threatened her and that McFuckhole dickwad. Who the hell do I think I am? Winston?

We do come from the same family. I guess it shouldn't surprise me that I'd make threats like that—and mean them.

Because I do mean it. That Morelli offshoot gets near my wife and I'll bash his face in. I don't even want him looking at her.

When I asked her if she gave him a blow job and she didn't say anything? I was fucking infuriated.

But I also walked right into that one. Don't ask questions you don't want to hear the answer to, and that's exactly what I did. To make things even better, I fucked her in the pool.

Without a condom.

What the hell was I thinking? What am I doing, putting everything at risk? We only just got married and now the potential is there that we've brought a baby into the mix? I'm too damn young.

So is she.

I barely know her.

This isn't a real marriage. The last thing we need to do is have a kid.

That's just all kinds of fucked up.

Watching her drag her eggs back and forth across the plate is literally driving me insane and I can't take it anymore.

"What the hell is wrong with you?" I yell.

She jumps, her fork falling with a clatter onto the plate as she glares at me. "You don't have to yell."

I soften my tone. "You're not eating."

"I'm not hungry."

"Still hungover?"

"A little. The headache's gone though," she admits, keeping her head bent. Like she can't look at me.

Guess I fucked it right out of her.

"You should eat," I demand and she does as I say, shoveling up the no doubt cold eggs and shoving them into her mouth.

The tension is thick, and I wonder if she's scared of me. She still won't look in my direction, and I suppose I deserve that. Her fear. Her resistance.

Wiping my mouth with the cloth napkin, I toss it on my empty plate and stand, leaving the table without another word. I drop my towel in the entryway, not really giving a fuck as I make my way to my bedroom and grab my phone, where I see I have a text from my brother.

Winston: *Call me as soon as you get this.*

I throw on a fresh pair of swim trunks and do as he asks.

"What's up?" is how I greet him when he says hello. "Find anything out yet?"

"A few details. We're still working on it." His voice is clipped, as if I'm already taking too much of his time and I blow out an exasperated breath.

I am sick of everyone's shit today.

"Give me what you've got, then."

"All right. McTiernan arrived in New York City last Friday morning. Flew in from Dublin and landed at JFK. Booked one of the cheapest rooms at the hotel where you were married."

I glance at my reflection in the mirror, wishing I could plow my fist through it. "He didn't fly in from Paris?"

"He's been back in Ireland for a while now. Not sure how long yet. Those details are still being hammered out."

"What else?"

"He checked out of the hotel Sunday morning and is now staying in Bishop's Landing."

Meaning he's also in Constantine territory. "Think he's a threat?"

"I don't know, but we can't assume he's not. I wouldn't be surprised if the Morellis will use him to try and talk to Charlotte and get information about us from her. The war between the Morellis and Constantines is over for some of us. With Lucian and Elaine. With Haley and Leo. But it's far from over for others." Winston pauses, and I know he's thinking about our cousin Haley's daughter. Squishy and loud but tolerable enough. And half of her blood is Morelli. Finding love has created a tenuous peace between our families. For now. "His ticket was one way."

"Fucking great," I practically growl. "So he'll be lingering around trying to talk to my wife indefinitely. If he's smart, he'll stay the fuck away from her."

"You don't sound pleased."

"I want him to back the fuck off."

"Why the hell do you care?"

I say nothing for a moment, unable to put into words what Charlotte means to me. Not that she actually means something.

As in, not that I love her, or care for her even. I'm attracted to her. We have chemistry. I like her sometimes.

And sometimes, I don't. I don't like her at all. I don't like that she dragged a Morelli into our lives and fucked everything up. Specifically I don't like that she dragged Seamus into our lives. He's a wild card. Dangerous to everything we've built. He's dangerous if he's working for the Morellis. And ironically he's even more dangerous if he's not.

Because then he'd be out of our reach.

Winston blows out a harsh breath. "Look, I get it. She's your wife now, and you want to protect her. There's something in the Constantine blood that turns us into raving lunatics when it comes to certain women."

"I want to rip his head off his neck with my bare hands," I mutter.

Winston actually chuckles, the dick. "These women of ours, they're a vulnerability. They make us do dumb shit. Impulsive, stupid shit."

I remember what he went through with Ash and the Morellis and those goddamn stepbrothers of hers. It was a nightmare, and he defended her honor right to the bitter end.

And he wasn't even married to her at the time.

Now he's got his own squishy, loud brat. My nephew Lane is named after our father.

"Let him know that, then," Winston suggests. "We can arrange a meeting when you get back. I think you two should meet."

I'm worried if I come face to face with that prick, I'll do something I'd regret—and end up in jail. "I don't know if that's a good idea."

"What else do you suggest? Listen, confronting him is the best way to get your intent across. Let him know he needs to back the fuck off. Imply what you might do if he gets too close."

I consider Winston's words, imagining a meeting with McPervert and what I might say to him. How he might react. What I'll have to do if he gives me any shit, which he probably will. It could destroy the tenuous peace between our families. And the tenuous peace in my new marriage. "I don't know."

"Think about it. It's the right move," Winston says with confidence.

"I'll figure it out when we get back home."

"I wouldn't wait too long if I were you." Winston pauses, changing the subject. "Enjoying your honeymoon?"

"It's been all right."

"The way you say it makes me think you're not getting any pussy."

Irritation blooms in my chest. "Don't talk about my wife like that."

Now my dickish brother is full-on laughing. "That tells me you're getting plenty of pussy. Have fun, little brother."

He ends the call before I can say anything else.

I drop my phone on the dresser and thrust both hands in my hair, gripping the back of my head as I glare at my reflection. I'm not handling this well. My conflicting emotions are all over the place and I can't get them under control. The woman is driving me out of my mind.

I like her. I don't.

I hate her. I don't.

I laugh with her. I want to wrap my hand around her throat.

I want to crush her.

I want to fuck her.

I just…

I want her.

Dropping my arms, I slip on a brand-new pair of Gucci slides that were packed in my luggage and head back outside to the pool, stopping short when I see that my wife had the same idea. She's stretched out on a lounger, her skin gleaming in the sun, giant sunglasses covering her eyes.

And that's the only thing she's wearing.

Shock courses through me as I continue to stare, taking in her luscious body I was fucking not even a half hour ago. Her entire body is on complete display and I don't know where to look first. She's got one knee bent, her foot flat on the cushion. Her long legs and pretty feet with the pale pink–painted toenails. Her breasts and the rosy-pink nipples. The flat curve of her stomach.

I scrub my hand along my jaw back and forth, telling myself to calm down. I can't do anything.

"I can feel you staring," she calls, her lips

barely moving. Hell, her body doesn't even move.

I drop my hand and rest both of them on my hips. "Pretty sure that's what you want."

"Actually, I wanted no tan lines."

"You put sunscreen on."

"No. Suntan oil."

"You'll burn."

"I'll risk it."

"You'll give yourself skin cancer."

"Again." She pauses, her lips curving into the slightest smile. "I'll risk it."

A ragged sigh escapes me. "I don't understand you at all."

"Who were you on the phone with?"

Something prickles over me, making me uneasy.

How'd she know I was on the phone?

"I could hear you talking," she says, as if she could hear my mental question. "Something about ripping someone's head off."

"I was talking to Winston."

She reaches for her sunglasses and pushes them into her hair, her blue eyes meeting mine. "About me and—"

"Don't say his name," I interrupt.

"Right." Her smirk is annoying as fuck. She tugs the glasses back over her eyes and tilts her face toward the sun, the movement making her breasts sway gently. "Nothing like a jealous husband to make your marriage kick off to a healthy start."

I curl my hands into fists. If that McAsshole was here right now, he wouldn't have a chance. "I'm not jealous."

She lowers her leg and now I can see her bare pussy. "Sure you're not."

This woman is unbelievable.

Like I have zero control, I go to her, settling myself on the edge of her lounger, reaching out to rest my hand on her knee. Her skin is hot from the sun. Smooth as silk. "Why would I be jealous when I could have this pussy any time I wanted?"

Charlotte lifts her glasses again, her gaze narrowed as she contemplates me. "You really think that?"

My fingers drift upward, from her knee to the inside of her thigh. I can feel the heat from her cunt and I itch to stroke her there. "I know I can. Why else would you sit outside like this? You're trying to bait me."

She slaps my hand away from her thigh. "No tan lines, remember?"

"Oh. Right." I nod, her sassy attitude a complete turn-on.

She's so full of shit.

I readjust myself on the lounger, pushing in between her legs so she has no choice but to spread them so wide her feet dangle over the sides.

Now she's on complete display. Pink, glistening flesh that's just begging for my mouth.

"So if I wanted to go down on you right now, you'd stop me?"

Her hand drops to her chest, her fingers drifting across the top of her breasts. I wish I could see her eyes. "Maybe."

"Uh-huh." I grab hold of her waist and tug her downward, bringing her closer to my mouth. She gasps, her nipples beading right in front of my eyes, and for the quickest moment, I wonder what the hell I'm doing.

And why.

Fuck it. I'm running on pure instinct. If I want to eat this pussy, I'm going to.

After all, she is my wife.

CHAPTER THIRTEEN

Charlotte

PERRY PULLS ME in closer, my legs spread wide open, showing him everything I've got. I guess I asked for this, lying out naked by the pool. What did I expect?

This, I think to myself as he strokes my hips. *Exactly this.*

He seems calmer. A little more contained than how he was earlier. When he was ferocious and territorial and ridiculous. I know I shouldn't think like this, but all that ragey intensity was kind of hot.

"Relax," he murmurs, his hands stroking downward, along my sides. Up and down.

He keeps gently stroking me and I can feel myself melting into the cushion. The warm breeze wafts over my hot skin, making everything inside of me ache and I lift my arms up, draping my wrists across the top of the lounger.

Keeping his grip on my hips, he leans in and brushes his mouth over my stomach, just above my navel. Everything inside of me clenches up tight at that first touch of his lips on my skin and I wait, all the air stuck in my throat, for him to shift lower.

He doesn't disappoint.

His mouth drifts down, just above my pussy, kissing and licking and nibbling. I squeal when he bites down hard enough to hurt and he sends me a look, his blue eyes blazing.

I tilt my hips up, giving him better access. The throbbing between my legs is incessant, filling my blood. My head. Until all I can think about is having his mouth on me.

Devouring me.

I don't know why he's doing this, but I don't complain. Maybe he's trying to apologize to me for being so horrible? Maybe he can't resist me?

I know it feels as if I can't resist him.

"Lift up," he murmurs and I do as he asks without hesitation. He slides his hands beneath my ass, his fingers teasing my crack as he drops a single kiss right on top of my pussy.

Right before he parts me with his fingers and lashes at my clit with his tongue.

I arch into his mouth, wanting to feel it everywhere, gripping the top of the lounger as I watch him search me thoroughly with his very talented tongue. The glasses are still on my face, allowing me to witness what he's doing to me without him being able to see my eyes and I kind of like it.

Oh God, I also really like what he's doing to me.

He's putting his whole face into it. Nuzzling me with his nose. His lips and tongue working me completely over. His big hands kneading my ass, splitting me wide open. I start to move with him, my gaze zeroed in on his tongue circling my clit. Flicking it. He glances up, as if he can feel my gaze on him and he never looks away as he continues to lick me. Putting on my own personal show.

His murmur of approval against my flesh has my skin humming in tandem and without thought I drop my hand on top of his head, keeping him with me. He dips his head, his eyes falling closed as he searches me thoroughly, no part of my pussy untouched by his magical tongue.

He doesn't let up for long, delicious minutes. His speed languid and slow at first, until he slowly but surely ratchets it up, his tongue working me over. He slips one finger inside my pussy, and then another, pumping them in and out.

I'm slowly but surely losing all control. Whimpering. Tossing my head back and forth. Closing my eyes. Opening them. Staring at the blue sky above, the palm trees gently swaying, the sound of the ocean in the near distance. If I could, I'd stay out here naked with my husband all damn day. As long as he kept doing this to me, I'd never want to put clothes on again.

A moan leaves me when he draws my clit between his lips and sucks. Hard. I'm mashing my pussy against his face, not even caring what I'm doing or how I look and I cry out in frustration when he pulls away from me.

"Flip over," he demands, the lower half of his face glistening with my juices.

I frown at him, so out of breath I can barely speak. "Wh-what?"

"Roll over." He grabs my hips and helps me along.

I do as he says, glancing around, unsure of what he's going to do next. I prop myself on my elbows, yelping when he jerks my legs apart. He rubs my ass cheeks with both hands, his touch rough, his hands slipping forward until they meet.

He spreads my ass cheeks apart and I can feel his gaze on me there. Embarrassment makes my cheeks burn and I glance over my shoulder to watch him bend down and lick my asshole.

"Oh!" The touch shocks. Sends a jolt of electricity straight through my body.

He does it again. Gentler this time. Searching. Exploring every part of me. When he moans against my flesh, I swear I can literally feel myself dripping onto the cushion.

He's enjoying this. Something that's so taboo, so filthy.

No one has ever done this to me before.

He continues licking me. Teasing me with his tongue until I'm thrusting back against his face, the impending orgasm roaring right back to life. Growing. Building into something big.

Bigger than I've ever experienced.

He shoves his fingers inside of my pussy and fucks me with them. A steady back and forth that has me rocking. His mouth still on my ass, his tongue licking my hole, God, it's too much.

It starts low in my belly and spreads outwards, until my entire body feels as if it's on edge, just dangling by a string.

"Come for me, baby," he murmurs against me and that's all it takes.

I'm coming, the shudders racking my body, his name falling from my lips. I'm vibrating, my heart racing so hard I swear I'm going to black out, and for a moment there, I think I actually do.

All the while he never lets up, his mouth busy on my flesh, his fingers pushing so deep inside of my body I swear he touches my womb.

Finally I come back to myself, the sound of the palm fronds fluttering in the wind. The heat from the sun soaking into my skin. My husband's face pressed against the back of my thigh as he rubs against it, his fingers now drifting across the ridged skin of my asshole.

A shiver moves through me when he tests me there, with just his fingertip.

I don't know if I can take any more. Despite the delicious tingles that sweep over me when he touches me like that.

My pussy throbs. My chest hurts. I slump against the lounger, my lips parted, the sunglasses falling off my face and onto the ground with a clatter. "Oh my God."

"Dirty girl," he murmurs against my right ass cheek, right before he kisses it. "I own you there."

I don't protest. He's right.

He does own me there.

And I'm sure he'll try to claim me in other

ways there as well.

✧ ✧ ✧

OUR RAUNCHY MOMENT in the sun left me golden. Guess the suntan oil worked, I think to myself as I step out of the outdoor shower and check my reflection in the steamy glass.

There are no tan lines to be found.

I lather myself up in body lotion, smoothing it everywhere I can reach. Until my newly golden skin is gleaming in the light. I grab one of the dresses Tinsley packed for me and slip it on, not bothering with panties or a bra.

There's something so liberating about being here. In Mexico, in this villa, with my husband. My entire body feels lit from within, and not just from the sun.

No, Perry has something to do with it. The way he seems to worship me with his hands and mouth and dick. Oh and his eyes. The way he watches me makes me feel powerful.

As if I could do anything.

That's a foreign experience for me. My entire life I've never felt powerful. My father controlled my every move. My older brothers snapped at me if I did something wrong. I went to a strict private school my younger years and was sent away to

Lancaster Prep as a freshman. Where lots of students tended to go wild and get into trouble, I stayed the course and kept my head down.

Meaning I was the complete opposite of the typical Lancaster.

I thought running away to Paris was my one shot at freedom but it turned into me letting another man control me.

Seamus.

With his lyrical accent and steely gaze. He moved with ease around the classroom, and spoke with such passion about the architectural history of Paris. I was enraptured. Crushing hard. And he knew it.

He took advantage of me, and I let him. I was totally swept up by his pretty words and suggestive glances. To the point that I basically threw myself at him in his cramped office at the university, sending his old desk chair backwards with a loud creak when I kissed him.

He kissed me back. That was the first sign something significant was going to happen between us. I was giddy. Obsessed.

I realize now he took advantage of a lonely, inexperienced girl. I was basically a child starved for affection, and somehow, he knew it. Sensed it.

And gave me everything I thought I wanted.

He controlled me and I didn't protest—I was used to it. Turned me into his dirty little secret and I never minded. There was something thrilling about sneaking around, reaching for each other in dark places, where no one would see. He'd slap my hand away if he thought I was getting too close in public, and that hurt.

He'd flirt with other women in class and that hurt too.

Yet he always had an explanation. A reason. I accepted those reasons, gullible and completely infatuated.

At one point, I thought it was love.

It all came crashing down that one afternoon in class. When he was in the middle of the lecture and a beautiful woman burst into the room, a giant smile on her face. Her dark hair flowed in flawless waves down her back and her dark eyes burned bright when they landed on him.

Her accent matched his. She threw her arms around his neck and kissed him soundly on the lips, making almost every single female in his classroom gasp with horror.

Including me.

She was his girlfriend. His fiancée. The woman he was going to marry. Meaning I was nothing.

Just a casual affair.

I never spoke to him again. I went back to my flat and cried into my pillow. I didn't go to class for a week, ignoring the emails from my instructors and the calls and texts from my newly made friends. One of my instructors eventually called my father, concerned for my welfare since I was such a good student.

My father demanded I come home and so I did. A shell of myself.

Completely devastated.

I eventually healed, and just when Seamus felt like a distant memory and I'd have no need to wonder about him ever again, he had to show his face.

And almost ruin everything.

"Hey." Perry knocks on the door three times, startling me. "You almost ready?"

We're going out to dinner, my husband and I.

"Almost," I call, reaching for the brush on the counter and running it through my damp hair. "Give me a few minutes."

He growls with frustration and walks away.

I glare at the door as if he can see my annoyance, hating the unease that slips over me. Sometimes it feels like he wants me and hates me, all at once, and I don't understand him.

At all.

After slicking my hair into a low ponytail, I contemplate putting on makeup but decide against it, only applying a pale pink lip balm before I rub my lips together and exit the bathroom. I slip on a pair of gold sandals and make my way out to the living room, where I find Perry clutching a drink in his hand as he stands at the window, staring out at the lit pool.

"I'm ready," I announce.

He turns, his hot gaze raking over me and I feel my nipples harden beneath my dress.

I wonder if he can tell. I wonder if he knows how much he affects me with just a look. A touch. I think of what he did to me earlier on that lounger and my cheeks burn.

Not with shame. With desire. I want him to do it again. I want to do so much more with my husband. Everything we possibly can.

"Nice dress," he says, not moving from his spot.

"Thank you." It's a pale blue and dotted with tiny red flowers. Soft and feminine with a flowing short skirt. If I twirl around in a circle, he might see that I'm not wearing any panties.

He looks nice too, clad in a pair of khakis and a white button-down shirt, the sleeves rolled up and showing off his forearms. That hint of a tattoo.

Sexy.

No rings or chains around his neck tonight though. His hair is tamed, his face clean shaven and he has the same golden tinge to his skin that I do.

The Mexico sun is good for us. We're glowing.

Or maybe it's from all the sex we're having.

Chapter Fourteen

Perry

We're playing a game, the wife and I. Throughout dinner she keeps sending me hot looks, as if she's imagining me naked. Or even better, she's reliving the moment we shared on the lounger earlier, when I licked her ass and made her come extra hard.

I called her a dirty girl and I meant it. She seemed to get off on that faster than anything else, which pleased me.

It's the only spot I feel like I own on her body and I'm going to fully claim it before the honeymoon is over. That is guaran-fucking-teed.

I send her hot looks too, enthralled with that sheen to her skin. How she seems to glow in the dim light of the restaurant. Her soft smiles and even softer laughter when I tell her something she deems funny, as if we share an inside joke.

Which I suppose we do. The joke's on everyone who thought we might hate this arrangement made between us. I'm still not one hundred percent down, but I've adapted.

That's one way to put it.

She's more careful with her alcohol tonight, merely sipping on a frothy margarita throughout the meal rather than gulping down one after the other. There's a difference to her, a confidence I don't think I've ever seen before, and damn it, it's fucking attractive.

I'm starting to realize I find everything my wife does is attractive.

"How's your lobster?" she asks me at one point, causing me to glance down at my mostly full plate. "You're not eating very much."

"I've got things on my mind," I admit.

Her plate is almost empty. "Trouble in paradise?"

"Ha ha." I down the straight tequila I requested earlier, the alcohol warm as it courses through my veins. Now I'm the one who wants to get drunk. But not so drunk I don't know what the fuck is going on.

I want the buzz when I fuck her later, because I'm going to.

Fuck her.

"Can I ask you a question?"

I shrug a shoulder. "You don't need my permission."

Her eyes blaze and I can tell she's pleased with my comment. This girl. I don't get her sometimes. "Why were you talking to Winston earlier?"

My entire body grows tense. "Business."

That's all I say.

A sigh leaves her. "That's what you all say."

"When you say all, who exactly are you referring to?" I ask. "And you better not say that dick's name."

"I'm not referring to him." She shakes her head. "I'm talking about my father. My older brothers. *Business* is always the answer when they don't want to tell you what's really going on."

Busted.

"I thought we were different, Perry. We're both young and just starting our lives. I'd hoped we could start off together," she continues.

"You sound delusional."

Her eyes narrow. "And you're rude. Can't you see I'm trying to be real with you right now? I know you don't want to talk about—*him*, but he's created a huge wall between us, and I wish you would just listen to me. When I first arrived in Paris, I was a young, sheltered girl who ended up being taken advantage of by a much older, more sophisticated man. He recognized that in me—my vulnerability. I had a crush, and he saw his opportunity."

My stomach churns. I do not want to hear this.

Yet I need to.

"You said you didn't want to talk about him during our honeymoon," I remind her.

She rolls her eyes. "When he's the ghost haunting our every move, we have to confront it, don't you think?"

I make a harumphing noise, sounding like an old man.

"When you were talking to Winston earlier, you said you wanted to rip someone's head off. Don't bother denying it," she says quickly when I part my lips, ready to protest. "I heard you, and you never answered me when I asked earlier. Whose head do you want to rip off?"

"Winston's," I automatically say.

She studies me, her expression impassive. "I don't believe you."

Damn it.

Can I trust her with the truth?

"It's none of your concern," I lie, and damn

it, my response only infuriates her.

"Are you going to keep secrets from me, Perry?" she throws at me.

"Are you going to keep secrets from *me*, Charlotte?" I throw back.

"I'm trying to open up, but it seems like you don't want to hear it."

We glare at each other, the air crackling between us. I can't reveal everything to her yet. What if she's actually talking to that McAsshat? What if she tells him everything I told her and he'll end up with the advantage?

I can't let her in on the family business information. Not yet. Maybe not ever. Most Halcyon information is confidential. If it fell into the wrong hands, it could cost plenty.

Maybe even everything.

"As a Lancaster, I'm bringing a lot of financial security to your family business," she says, sounding haughty as fuck. "I have every right to know what's happening. What decisions are being made. Especially if any of my family's money is being used in those business decisions."

"We're not using your family's money to fund our business dealings," I snap.

She grabs her glass and drains it, slamming it down onto the table extra hard. "Then why did you marry me?"

"For the name. For the connections. For the reach. Your family has been around for generations. Hundreds of years. The Lancaster influence is unmatched." That's how Winston explained it to me. We don't necessarily want their money.

Not yet, anyway.

We need their name to open doors and introduce us to even bigger players. Larger corporations. Halcyon will eventually be on a global level the likes that no one else has ever seen.

Certainly not any goddamn Morellis.

"We're nothing but a business merger." Her voice is flat.

It feels like she's testing me. As if she's looking for me to confirm that we're something else. Something more.

Are we?

No. Not really. The sex is just a bonus. She's reading too much into it.

Just like a woman would.

"You knew this from the start," I murmur, leaning back in my chair. Needing the distance. Anger blasts off her in a wave of heat, making me sweat. And I'm not in the mood.

I'd rather sweat tonight in other ways.

"You feel nothing for me."

"I like fucking you."

She flinches. "You're an asshole."

"Charlotte." I lean forward once more, resting my forearms on the table. "You're a Lancaster. I've done the research. You come from a long line of ruthless assholes."

"I'm a woman. The Lancaster women are different. We feel too much to make up for the men's lack of emotion. I don't have sex with you just because it feels good. And it feels really, really good, what you do to me."

"Even earlier?" I raise a brow. I was cruel the first round. And crude the second.

"I should say no. I should say I found it offensive and almost borderline assault."

What the fuck?

"But that would be a lie," she continues. "I enjoyed every second of it and am counting the minutes until we can do it again."

My cock surges to life at her confession.

"This is me being honest with you, Perry. I don't want to lie to you. And I don't want you to lie to me either." She's quiet for a moment. Assessing.

My wife is smart. She's using our sexual connection to get me to be truthful with her.

But I'm just as smart.

"You're a hot fuck, wife. I can't lie about that." I wipe the smile off my face with my hand, being purposely callous.

The hurt in her gaze is unmistakable. She stares at me, her eyes glassy and she suddenly leaps to her feet, tossing her napkin on top of her plate.

"Fuck you," she mutters before she walks away.

Leaving me alone at the table.

"Damn it," I whisper as I stand, about to chase after her but I'm stopped by the server who wants me to sign for our bill. I do as he requests, irritated enough that I give him a lesser tip for holding me up before I'm out of the restaurant and chasing after my wife.

She's far ahead of me, running in those gold heels, her skirt flaring up with the breeze and I swear to God was that her bare ass I just saw?

The skirt flips up again, and yep, there are her naked golden cheeks.

Picking up the pace, I run after her, drawing closer. I call her name but she doesn't acknowledge me.

Charlotte just keeps running.

Only when she's stuck at the villa trying to open the front door with the key card that I catch her. I pin her to the door with my body, my front pressed against her back and she hangs her head, trying to nudge me away with a not so friendly push of her ass.

It doesn't work. All it does is remind me that she's naked beneath the dress and my cock stands at attention.

"I hate you," she says, still facing the door. Like she can't bear to look at me. "Stop trying to win me over with sex. I'm not interested."

I run my hand over her hip, my fingers carefully gathering up the soft fabric, until just the bottom of her ass cheeks are exposed. I slip my hand beneath the hem, skimming my fingers over her smooth skin, dipping them between her legs.

She's wet. Hot.

"Not interested," I say as I slowly begin to stroke her. "Right."

"I hate you." Her voice trembles and she hangs her head.

"I hate you too, babe." I press my cock against her so she can feel how much I can't stand her. "Now are we going inside, or do I have to fuck you on the doorstep?"

Charlotte blows out an aggravated breath, pressing her forehead against the door. "Fuck me out here, then. I dare you."

For whatever weird reason, it's exactly what I

want to hear. Without hesitation, I've got my cock out in seconds, her skirt is pushed up and I'm sliding inside of her, groaning low when I feel all that creamy heat wrap tightly around me. She whimpers, arching her back and sending me deeper and I glance around, making sure no one is out here.

We're fairly isolated but I can see a few other villas in the near distance. The pathways are lit, and an employee or, hell, even a guest could go walking by at any moment. We're not completely alone out here.

Maybe that's half the thrill.

I grab hold of her hips and start fucking her, my gaze zeroed in on the spot where my cock visibly slides in and out of her pussy. Damn it, that's hot. Can't get enough of it. Her legs are spread wide and she's bent almost in half, her face still pressed against the door, her moans growing louder and louder.

I move faster, already close. This woman makes me come too quickly and I don't like it. It's as if I get inside her and I lose all control.

Like now.

"Don't you dare come inside me," she says when I stiffen, her voice accusatory. "You're not wearing a condom."

Smart catch. Always observant, my Charlotte.

I thrust harder, a groan leaving me when I feel her clench those inner walls around my shaft, as if she's trying to squeeze the orgasm out of my cock. It fucking works because the next thing I know, I'm pulling out of her, coming all over her ass, coating her skin with my semen.

She's breathing hard, her body still bent, her eyes meeting mine as she glares at me over her shoulder. She's furious. She's beautiful.

She needs to come.

I run my fingers through my semen and smear it against her pussy, finding her clit and rubbing it. She whirls around to face me and I curl my other hand around her, lifting her up, her legs coming around my waist.

Her cunt is so wet I can hear it when I rub her clit with my come-coated fingers. She never looks away from me as I stroke her faster. Harder. Her breaths seem to lock up in her throat, her body trembling, her eyes growing hazy. Until she tilts her head back, a soft cry falling from her lips when the orgasm hits.

She's shaking. I grip her closer, my fingers still busy on her clit. Fuck, she's hot when she comes. Her body undulates against mine, her nipples poking against the fabric of her dress and I pin her against the door with my body, reaching for the neckline and tugging it down so I can draw a nipple into my mouth.

"Oh God," she gasps, her hand coming around the back of my head as she holds me to her. "Don't stop."

I don't. I keep sucking and licking her nipple, stroking her pussy until it must hurt, but she never tells me to quit. In fact, she comes again. A smaller one this time, and hearing her cry out, feeling her body react to my attention, has my cock hard as a fucking rock to the point that I'm in pain.

"We're going inside," I growl against her lips when her breathing has eventually slowed. "And I'm going to fuck you again."

"Okay."

"Even if you hate me."

"I do." She swallows. "Hate you."

"Enough to suck my cock?"

"Only if you lick me again like you did earlier."

"You mean your asshole?"

She nods.

"Say it," I whisper against her still trembling lips. "Say what you want me to do to you, Charlotte."

"I want you to fuck me, Perry," she whispers, her lips parting when mine land on hers, her tongue darting out. I suck it, letting it go so she can continue. "I want you to lick my asshole."

"Filthy fucking wife," I murmur, smiling. "Maybe I'll fuck your sweet little asshole too."

She devours me when I say that, and I let her.

Who knew hate sex could feel so fucking good?

CHAPTER FIFTEEN

Charlotte

I ROLL OVER onto my stomach, clutching my pillow in my arms, my eyes tightly closed against the streaming sunlight. The spot next to me is empty—I'm back in my own bed, alone and exhausted. My muscles ache. I hurt…everywhere.

All thanks to my husband and the marathon sex session we had last night. This morning. Only a couple of hours ago.

There was no actual anal sex involved yet—but he did just about everything else he could to my poor, tender ass. To the point he knew he couldn't push me any further.

He used his fingers. His lips. His tongue. He penetrated me and made me cry out, my body clenching tight around his finger, scared to allow him to go further. Until he eventually gave up, though not without a fight.

And not without making me come either. God, it feels so good when he touches me like that. It also feels incredibly taboo, but he's convincing me it's really not.

The man is very, *very* convincing.

At one point he told me he was addicted to my pussy and I tend to believe him. He can't leave the damn thing alone.

I feel the same way about him.

We are already on day three of this five-day honeymoon and I'm a little sad that it's going by so quickly. Soon we'll have to return home. Back to reality and more secrets and lies. I tried to get him to open up with me and be truthful last night at dinner, but it was pointless. He clammed up, making me furious.

He's not going to tell me anything about his business or whatever it was he and Winston were talking about on the phone yesterday. I get the sneaking suspicion he was talking about me. And Seamus.

That's whose head he wants to rip off. My ex-lover's. I should find that ridiculous and territorial, but deep down, that's not how I feel at all.

I like it. I want him to feel protective of me. And not because of business dealings or whatever. I want him to protect me because he cares.

Because I'm valuable to him—as a person, not a commodity.

I don't know if that's a pipe dream, but I can't help wanting it.

Eventually I drag my tired ass out of bed and take a quick shower. Throw on a new bikini—this one hot pink with bottoms so skimpy most of my ass hangs out—and head for the kitchen, where I can smell coffee brewing.

I'll need as much caffeine as possible to get through this day.

When I enter the airy kitchen, I realize my husband isn't there. I pour myself a cup and add a little creamer, going to the massive window above the sink that overlooks the backyard, and that's where I spot him.

Clad only in tropical-print swim trunks, pacing back and forth, his phone clutched to his ear. He's talking animatedly, gesturing with his free hand, his voice rising and falling. As if he's angry. I can hear the muffled sounds of his side of the conversation, but I can't quite make out what he's saying.

Fortifying myself with a few sips of coffee, I set my cup on the counter and go to the slider, opening the door so his voice comes through loud and clear.

"...the plane will be available tomorrow, then? Good. We need to get on this." His gaze lifts, meeting mine and his entire demeanor shifts, just like that. He looks away from me, growling into the phone, "I gotta go. I'll call you later." A pause. "Right."

Disappointment leaves my heart heavy. I already know he's going to tell me we're leaving tomorrow. Only one more day with him in paradise.

Only one more day left that I have to convince him he can trust me with his business secrets. His personal secrets.

His everything.

"Hey," he greets me once he ends the call. "You sleep well?"

"For all of two hours," I answer, trying my best not to ask what that phone conversation was about. "How about you?"

"Didn't really sleep at all," he admits.

"Oh? Why's that?"

"Too much on my mind." His gaze roams over me, lingering on his favorite spots. "Nice suit."

"You like?" I pull the sliding glass door shut behind me and start to approach him, but I can barely make the walk.

The pool deck is too hot and I don't have shoes on.

Yelping, I go back to the shallow end of the pool and hop into the cool water, sighing with relief. Annoyed with myself that I can't make a sexy walk toward my husband without burning the soles of my feet.

Perry just laughs at me, and at least he seems cheery. Not all stern and serious like he was on the phone.

"Who were you talking to?" I ask, gasping when he jumps into the deep end, making such a splash, my face is immediately covered with water droplets. I'm sure he didn't hear me.

Or he's going to pretend he didn't.

He pops up in the shallow end, directly in front of me, a faint smile on his face as he grips my hips, toying with the straps of my bikini bottoms with his fingers. I'm still on the top step, so I hover above him. "Let's go exploring today, wife."

"What do you want to explore?" I settle my hands on his shoulders, squeezing him. Loving how broad he is. How solid.

And how easygoing he's acting right now. As if we're a perfectly normal married couple having fun on their honeymoon.

What a crock of shit.

"Around the resort. They have a few things going on. There's a trail we could hike."

I scowl. "I'm from the city. I don't hike."

He laughs. "Learn how to surf?"

"In one day?" I raise a brow. "I doubt I could manage it."

"It would be fun to watch you fall repeatedly in the water."

"You're mean," I murmur, running my hand through the damp hair curling at his nape. "Why are you being so nice to me?"

Perry is quiet for a moment before he lets loose a ragged sigh. "We have to return home tomorrow."

"Why?" I want him to tell me the truth. Not some vague bullshit answer.

"Something's—come up. I'll explain it later." He tugs on my hips, pulling toward him so we're treading water together, our legs tangling. "Let's just have fun today. Before we go back to hating each other."

I'm such a liar when I tell him I hate him. It's more that I hate what he's doing. What he's saying. I don't actually hate *him.*

No, something worse is happening.

I'm actually starting to care about him.

Far too much.

✧ ✧ ✧

IN THE END, we indulge each other for the afternoon. I sit out on the beach and soak up the sun while he learns how to surf with last-minute lessons. He is of course, great at it. He gets up on the board almost immediately, and rides a couple of waves that I can't help but find completely terrifying. The instructor keeps hooting and hollering, encouraging Perry to do more daring stuff.

All while I sit there and chew on my thumbnail, nervous he might hurt himself.

Watching Perry out in the water is giving me a glimpse to another side of him that I knew existed, but never actually witnessed before. He's a complete daredevil. Spontaneous and not afraid of anything. Like, every single thing the instructor asks him to do, he does it. No questions asked.

"Be careful!" I shriek at one point, when he's so far out on the water he's just a little blip on a surfboard, a giant wave coming at him. I'm positive he couldn't hear me.

It didn't matter—I needed to yell just to get out some of my panic. My heart felt like it was going to beat out of my chest and panic clawed at my insides. I didn't want anything bad to happen to him.

And I can't analyze why I care so damn much.

By the time he's finished with his lesson, I'm a mess, barely keeping my composure. I've got my arms wrapped around my bent legs and I'm shivering despite the heat as Perry makes his way over to me. His smile is wide and his muscular body is still dripping wet and oh God he is so incredibly sexy.

I'm also mad at him for putting his life at risk like that. I don't know if my heart can take much more of that.

"Wasn't that amazing?" He grins, looking pleased with himself.

"You caught on fast." My voice is tight.

He doesn't even notice, plopping down on the ground next to me, his skin automatically covered in sand. "It was such a rush out there. I fucking loved it."

I'm glad someone loved it. I could barely stand watching him.

"You're turning pink," he observes, his fingers skimming my shoulder, making me tremble. "Soon you'll be as bright as the suit you're wearing if you don't watch it."

I scowl at him. "I used sunscreen."

"You might need more." He turns away from me and props his hands into the sand behind him, tilting his head back and closing his eyes. I study him, marveling yet again at how handsome he is. How loose and relaxed he seems right now. The surfing might've led to a near heart attack for me, but it seems to have completely calmed him down. "I feel good. This trip has been…nice."

A mild way to put it.

"Yes," I murmur, sliding my fingers in the sand right next to him. I wish I could touch him freely. Drift my fingers across his thigh. Tuck a single finger beneath the loose waistband of his swim trunks. Would he mind? Or would he think it weird?

I decide not to test it.

"Very nice," I finish when I realize he seems to be waiting for more of a response from me. "I've had a—good time."

"Me too." He angles his head toward me, his lips curved. "I've learned a lot."

"Same."

He chuckles. "What the hell are we doing, Charlotte?"

"I don't know," I admit, loving how real we're being in this moment. "Let's not overanalyze it. Our day is almost over."

"We leave tomorrow at ten," he says, his voice soft.

My heart pangs. Less than twenty-four hours until we have to go home. "That's so soon."

"Too soon." He doesn't hesitate when he reaches for me, tangling his fingers in my hair and tucking a few loose strands behind my ear. "I like you like this. Half-naked and watching me show off."

"Perry."

"What?" He caresses my cheek, his touch featherlight. "I can tell you want to touch me, wife."

"Us Lancasters aren't very touchy people," I admit. "We never really have been."

"Oh yeah?" He leans in so his mouth is level with my ear. "Well, you've been touching me a lot lately."

Sometimes he makes it so easy.

"You don't mind?"

He pulls away frowning. "Why would I mind? I like it."

"You do?"

"Yeah. I like the way you look at me too." His gaze locks with mine. "I was putting a show on for you out there, and it seemed like you were eating it up."

I burst out laughing. "You scared the crap out of me."

He frowns. "I did? Really?"

Nodding, I give in to my urges and slip my finger into the side of his swim trunks, tugging on the waistband. "You're reckless."

"I get so into it I don't even think about anything else. I used to do that when I'd race cars," he admits.

"I want to hear about that sometime," I tell him, meaning every word I say. "Maybe you could tell me about it tonight. Over dinner."

"You really want to know?"

I nod. I want to know everything about him, not that I could ever admit that out loud.

"I should show you the Chevelle," he continues, his gaze turning hazy. As if he's thinking about his car and how much he adores it, which is kind of cute. "I love that fuckin' thing. I miss it."

"When we get back home, you should take me for a ride," I suggest.

"Everyone hates that car," he says immediately, on the defensive. "She's bright orange. The muffler is loud. Winston thinks it's stupid."

"I don't think it's stupid." My voice is soft. I'm trying to tell him without saying out loud that I don't think anything he does is stupid.

Well…mostly.

"You haven't even seen her yet."

"Anything that you enjoy, I want to like too," I admit.

"Aw. Aren't you sweet." His smile is soft, and when he leans in and kisses me, I almost believe he means it.

Almost.

CHAPTER SIXTEEN

Perry

I MADE A mistake. I should've never told Winston I wanted to come home early after he shared more details the investigative team told him about Seamus McDicklick, and that I was considering meeting up with the asshole too.

Why do I care what that guy is doing back at home when I've got what he wants with me in Mexico? And damn, do I have her. Every which way I can.

After spending hours with her last night into this morning exploring every little bit of her sexy body and trying my damnedest to get inside her tight ass—that's hopefully going to happen tonight—I was exhausted. I should've fallen into a deep sleep and woken up around noon.

But I couldn't sleep. I couldn't stop thinking about Charlotte. And her ex-lover. All the things they must've done together. All those firsts he got to steal from me.

I hate him so damn much. He haunts my fucking nightmares. Though they're not necessarily bad dreams.

They're always bad for him. Last night, I dreamed about meeting up with Seamus at Halcyon. He wouldn't stop taunting me, eventually saying something so incredibly stupid I end up smashing his face in with my fist. I then called security to escort him out of my office while he glares at me, one eye swollen shut thanks to the beating he took.

I've beat his ass in a variety of ways every night since I got married.

It's easier to not sleep at all, so I didn't. Instead, I sent a string of texts to my brother demanding to know what's going on and played fucking Candy Crush on my phone until I finally heard back from him.

The information wasn't much, but it was enough to spur me on to get back home and back to business. I want that asshole out of my and Charlotte's life for good. I don't need him lurking around and trying to use her to get to me. To us.

To our family.

Still can't get over the Morellis thinking they

could interfere with my marriage and get Charlotte to talk, giving up any secrets she might know.

Do they really think I'm that stupid? That I'd give up confidential Halcyon information to my new bride?

Shit, maybe they do.

And that enrages me even more.

Then again, maybe it's not the Morellis acting as a whole. They've already split into factions. Lucian runs Morelli Holdings now, not his father. And word is that Vincent never accepted his brother's inheritance. Maybe I'm part of some kind of power struggle, and McTiernan is a soldier in that war.

Spending time with her on the beach this afternoon was the distraction we both needed. Though I realized after my surf lesson that I really put her through it, watching me out there on the water. I can admit sometimes I'm a little too reckless. It's why I stopped racing. It's why I garaged the Chevelle. Something about that car makes me feel invincible, when I'm not.

I need to remember that.

Being on the surfboard gave me the same feeling. I took to it quick—didn't bother telling Charlotte I had lessons on another family vacation in Mexico long, long ago, when my father was still alive—and swimming out there, riding those waves, I felt like a goddamn superhero. Such an adrenaline rush.

Almost as good as sex with my wife.

After coming back from the beach, we each took a nap in our respective beds before we got ready to have dinner with a view of the sunset. I decide to dress up a little extra since it's our last night and we're eating at the most expensive restaurant at the resort.

I'm going all out. Hopefully Charlotte is too. Seeing her come out in a different dress, bikini, whatever she's wearing each day has been a worthwhile surprise. One I've enjoyed immensely.

Hell, I've enjoyed this entire trip. We've come to an unspoken agreement. I still don't fully trust her, and I'm sure she feels the same about me. Sometimes I don't like how she makes me feel either.

I'd guess she also feels the same.

We're forgetting all about that today, though. Tonight. We're just going with the flow and enjoying each other. Reality will catch up with us when we return home, and we can also resume our obvious distrust with each other too.

Can't wait.

I decide to layer on the rings and the chains. Leave a couple of extra buttons undone on my cream-colored shirt. My hair is looking good. I've got a nice tan thanks to all the time I've spent in the sun. And despite the lack of sleep last night, I still manage to look rested.

I'm waiting for Charlotte in the living room, checking my inbox when she finally walks in, an unsure expression on her face.

"I'm overdressed," she says.

I take in her dress. It's a deep, rosy pink. With flimsy straps and a deep V in the front that shows off her tanned skin—and her tits. The skirt is short and made of three layers of thin fabric and all I can see is her legs and her skin and I immediately want to know if she's got panties on underneath.

My guess is no.

"You're not overdressed," I reassure her as I rise from the couch and go to where she's standing. I stop directly in front of her, resting a hand on her waist, my gaze eating her up. "You're fucking beautiful."

Her smile is small. Pleased. "Thank you. You look nice too."

"Ready to go?" I ask.

She nods. "Let's do it."

This woman is speaking my language.

I hope to be doing it with her all night long.

✧ ✧ ✧

THE MEN IN the restaurant can't stop staring at my wife and I can't stop glaring at them. I had no idea her in that dress would cause such an uproar, but I underestimated Charlotte.

She's stunning, and they all know it.

I didn't even realize until I was sitting across from her at the table that she was wearing the earrings I gave her as a wedding present. She tucked her hair behind her ear, the diamonds twinkling in the light and a surge of unfamiliar emotion made my chest tight.

This woman belongs to me. I keep repeating the thought in my brain and out loud, specifically to her, and I know I sound like some sort of caveman who beats his chest with his fists, but fuck.

She brings out a primitive side to me I didn't know I had. And I keep thinking about it because it keeps hitting me over and over again, what I've done.

What we've done.

I got married. To a woman I didn't know, but I'm starting to actually like.

Yes, before the wedding I had those protective urges surge up that made me demand we move in together, but that was different. I just wanted to get her away from her father. I'm the type of guy who wants to protect people. I've run to the rescue of my little sister countless times. I help out where I can. I like feeling useful.

Considering I'm the second son and the obviously favored child of my mother, I never felt particularly useful growing up. I was just there. Yet another Constantine among many.

Winston eventually gave me my shot at Halcyon and I proved to him I could be an asset to the company. I agreed to marry a stranger to help the family—and Charlotte. She needed to get out of her situation and I didn't mind being the one to assist.

Even if it costs me my relationship freedom. Hell, before we got married, she mentioned more than once she'd run away, and eventually, I could divorce her. Or we could even have it annulled. Her leaving would break all sorts of clauses in the contract and her father would probably have to pay my mother an outrageous amount of money, but would it really matter to him, beyond the humiliation? Not like the payment would hurt him.

The man is worth billions.

At least Charlotte would be free.

But as I stare at her while she scoops up ceviche with a giant tortilla chip, shoving it into her mouth and humming her approval, I don't know if I want her to run away from me anymore.

I want to keep her.

Exhaling, I reach for my drink and slam it down, needing the alcohol to clear my head. I'm thinking like a crazy man. I can't *keep* her. She's not something I can own, not really. Charlotte is a human being with thoughts and feelings and opinions who can exert her free will in any way she wants. I may get all territorial with her, but in the end, I will never make her do something she doesn't want to do.

Like stay with me.

If she hates me that much, if she feels the need to flee that strongly, I'll let her go.

I'm not a dick.

"You're so quiet tonight," she observes.

I glance up to find her watching me, her blue eyes wide and unblinking. Swear to God her hair is blonder and her eyes are brighter against her golden skin. That pink dress fits her to perfection and my gaze drops to her chest. The tops of her tits. I want to touch her there. Kiss her there.

"Are you tired?" she asks when I still haven't said anything.

"A little," I admit.

The disappointment is clear on her pretty face. She's not wearing much makeup, which I prefer. She was beautiful at our wedding, but I like her natural. With her guard down and her face clean. Her lips are pink and glossy and I think that's the only cosmetics she has on.

"You'll probably want to go to bed early," she says.

I stare at her. She must be out of her mind.

"Probably not."

A smile curves her lips and she grabs another tortilla chip, dunking it into the ceviche before she pops it into her mouth. "Tell me about cars," she says after she's swallowed.

Unease filters through me and I shift in my seat. No one else cares about me and cars. I raced in secret, never telling my mother or siblings. Winston found out by accident after I quit, and he was furious. Claimed I had a million-dollar life insurance policy on my head and our enemies could've found out and killed me.

I couldn't help but think hey, at least they could've gotten a cool mill for my death, but I decided that wouldn't be the best thing to say to my brother at the time.

"What do you want to know?"

"How you started street racing. That's so—random." She wrinkles her nose, looking adorable. "Though after watching you surf earlier, I'm realizing that you enjoy participating in…reckless activities."

"Aw, do you disapprove, wife?" I'm teasing her.

"I don't disapprove, it was just scary, watching you out there. You didn't have a lot of experience surfing yet you approached those waves as if you've been doing it your entire life," she says.

"I wasn't that good." I really wasn't. I think I made her panic, is all.

"The surfing doesn't matter. Tell me about the cars. And racing."

I lean back in my chair, contemplating how much I want to tell her. It's hard to part with your secrets when you've held them so close for so long.

"It began a few years ago. Even before I got the Chevelle. I was hanging out with these guys I went to high school with and they would go watch this giant group of illegal street racers. They'd announce the location where the races would happen via social media and all in code.

Always in the middle of the night, when the streets were mostly empty and the cops wouldn't be around," I explain.

"So you started out watching."

"And knew immediately I wanted to race," I tell her. "I got to know some of the guys, and eventually, they let me join them. First race I participated in, I won."

"Of course you did."

I laugh. "It was such a fucking rush, I knew I had to keep doing it. And I did—kept winning, too. I bought the Chevelle, and fuck that baby did so damn well racing. There is nothing better than racing with a five-speed and that engine? V-8, baby." I'm getting excited like I usually do when I talk about my precious orange baby.

"Sounds like you were having fun," she says.

"It was fun. But it was dangerous too." Real dangerous. But I didn't care. It was like I had a death wish. Who did I need to live for? Speed, that was it. That's all I sought. I threw my all into work during the day and racing at night. I had the Chevelle modified. I went on YouTube and studied the guys I was racing. I'd lose as much as I won and that frustrated me.

I wanted to win.

All the time.

"What made you stop?" Her voice is soft, and when I meet her gaze, I see the interest there. And the worry.

This woman gets it. I can just tell. Her worry doesn't even bother me. It makes me feel as if she cares.

"It was a Saturday night. And I was going to be in a big race against a complete psycho." And I mean that. Ernie Portello is a known street racer who flat-out does not give a fuck. He's had so many near misses and actual accidents, it's a miracle he's still alive.

He's still racing too, while I quit like a coward.

"Does he have legit mental problems? Or are you just saying that?" she asks.

"I'm pretty sure the guy is undiagnosed. He has to have something wrong with him. No one behaves like he does." I shake my head, remembering past races I watched with Ernie always the winner.

I wanted to beat him. No one else could. I planned on being the first.

"What happened? Did you race him?"

I nod, tracing the rim of my glass. I need another drink. "Yeah. We were the final race of the night, and we switched locations at the last minute because the police were coming. Someone ratted us out."

I found out later it was an inside job. One of Ernie's men called it in so we'd have to move.

"Had you raced at the new location before?"

"Nope." I shake my head. "He already had the advantage."

"Someone made that happen," she states, her voice flat, her gaze fiery. "They did that on purpose to trip you up."

"You're a smart one, wifey." I tap my temple, smiling faintly. "At the time, I didn't give a shit. I was ready to get it on and pissed that the race was postponed in the first place. We always have a team when we do this, you know? Your guys that watch out for you, makes sure the car is good. That you're good. Every dude on my team told me not to do it. I ignored them."

Charlotte rests her elbow on the table and props her chin on her fist, seemingly enraptured. "What happened next?"

I blow out a low breath before I launch into retelling the scariest night of my life. "At first it was easy. I jumped ahead almost immediately and I remember thinking he was holding back, but I blew the thought off. I was such a cocky son of a bitch that I actually believed I had it in the bag."

I'm quiet for a moment and I can feel the nerves radiating from Charlotte, even across the table. And the race already happened. Here I sit, alive to tell the tale.

Yet she's still anxious for me.

"There was an unexpected hairpin turn. It was sharp. To the right. Came up on me so quickly, I took it too fast and spun the fuck out. He pulled past me and won. He was going slower because he knew that turn was there and I didn't. He knew he couldn't take me on a straightaway. I was fucking good, Charlotte. So good. Until that race. It messed with my confidence. I gave up after that."

"Were you hurt?"

"Just—scared." It was hard to admit that. How terrifying that moment was. How my life flashed before my eyes when I lost complete control of the car. Like an idiot, I worried first for the Chevelle.

Then I worried for me.

"How about the car?"

"It had some minor body damage."

She frowns. "How come?"

"I swung the back end into a pole. A streetlight." Once that happened, and after Ernie won the race, everyone bailed. Even my own team. No one wanted to get busted by the police. I couldn't blame them for scattering like cockroaches, but damn.

I had to deal with the repercussions that night all alone. I couldn't even call my family. I didn't want to freak them out or worry about me. More than anything, I didn't want any of them to give me a lecture and tell me what to do.

"Was the damage bad?"

"Fixable." The server appears with our dinner and I make conversation with the guy, needing the distraction.

I don't like thinking about that night, and what happened.

It reminds me that I'm mortal. And that's the last thing I want to remember.

CHAPTER SEVENTEEN

Charlotte

PERRY WAS QUIET for the rest of our dinner. Not necessarily in a bad mood, but rather pensive. In his head. He didn't eat much but drank plenty and seeing him like this made me lose my appetite too.

My husband isn't feeling so great. I can see it in his eyes, and the faint strain around his mouth. The tightness of his jaw. Telling that story about his racing days put him in a foul mood and that is the last thing I want for our last night here.

But there's no getting him out of it. I try to joke. I try to flirt. I fail miserably at both things, and eventually, I give up. I may think I know him, but I don't. Not fully. We still have a long way to go before I can feel confident around this man.

On the walk back to our villa, I contemplate

the many ways I could possibly seduce him. Something I've never really done before, but I'm willing to put myself out on a limb for my husband. So far, everything I do he seems to like. Even when he's furious with me, he still wants me, which is kind of hot.

Twisted and a little sick, but still hot.

He's not mad at me tonight though. He's lost in his memories and quiet. Maybe even a little bit down. I refuse to be one of those women who asks, *what's wrong?* That gets you nowhere. I've witnessed that enough between my parents, when my mother would repeatedly ask my father that question until he finally blew.

No, thank you.

Someone needs cheering up though.

I reach for Perry's hand, interlocking our fingers and he doesn't let go. I sway our locked hands so our arms swing and he glances over at me, his brows lowered. "You okay? A little drunk maybe?"

I shake my head, deciding to be truthful. "Trying to cheer you up."

"I'm in a shit mood, huh." He squeezes my hand.

I squeeze back. "A little."

"I don't like thinking about that night."

I appreciate his honesty, and I feel bad too.

"I probably shouldn't have asked."

"No, I don't mind that. I just—I don't talk about it much because it brings me down. I was stupid. I let my ego get in the way and almost cost myself my life." He shakes his head, his gaze finding mine. "I've made some mistakes."

"You'll keep making them too," I remind him.

He chuckles. "Nothing like keeping it real, huh?"

"I'm just being honest." I shrug.

Perry's quiet again, and am I too. I enjoy the walk. The salty scent of the ocean mixed with the sweet smell of the tropical flowers growing nearby. In the near distance I hear laughter. Someone having a good time, enjoying their vacation while I'm slowly but surely filling with impending doom.

Our trip is almost over and we're back to reality. To secrets and lies and Seamus lurking around. The distrust from my husband and his family. The lack of support from mine.

What will I do when we go home? Camp out in that apartment my parents gave us and hang out with Jasper and Doja? Is that all I'll ever amount to? Would Perry mind if I tried to go to college or would he think I'll try and have an affair with another professor?

The idea of that hurts. More than I care to admit.

"Maybe I am wiped," Perry finally says as we draw closer to the villa.

My hopes for an adventurous night with Perry come crashing down around me. "You didn't get much sleep last night."

"I got none. Plus, I still need to pack before we leave in the morning."

"I do too," I admit.

We slowly walk up the front steps, our hands still linked until Perry reaches for the key card in his pants pocket. He unlocks the door and we enter the villa, turning toward each other when the door shuts.

"Thank you for sharing that story with me," I say, wanting him to know how much it meant to me, even though hearing the details made my heart hurt.

"Thanks for listening. I've never told anyone what happened that night before," he confesses.

I'm shocked. "No one?"

He shakes his head.

"Not even your mother?"

"Oh hell no, I could never tell her. She'd flip

the fuck out." He smiles, and then it's gone. Scrubbed away by the hand he runs over his mouth. "I'm gonna crash out in my room."

Disappointment fills me and I try to push it aside.

"Okay." I follow him until we separate at the mouth of the hallway. His bedroom is on one end and mine is on the other. "Good night."

He yanks me in for a quick hug, pressing his lips to my forehead before he lets me go. "Night, wife. Sleep tight."

"You too." I offer him a little smile and scurry down the hall and into my room, shutting the door with a quiet click, leaning against it.

I slowly bang the back of my head on the door, annoyed at myself. Why didn't I suggest we spend the night together? Even if all we did was sleep, it would be a good way for us to get closer.

And that's what this honeymoon did. It brought us closer. I understand him more now, and I hope he understands me. Though I blabbed all of my problems to him before we got married, so maybe he was beginning to understand me even then.

Yet he still went through with it. He married me.

Does he think I'm going to end things like I

told him I would at the beginning of our bogus engagement? I meant what I said then. I couldn't stand the thought of marrying a stranger and having to live with him, but when I spent a little time with Perry, I realized he wouldn't be so bad. Better than living under the tyrannical rule of my father.

Though almost anyone is better than living with Reginald Lancaster.

Perry hasn't brought my leaving up, but I hope he's not counting on me doing that. I'm starting to think I don't want to.

No, I *know* I don't want to leave him. I like him. I care about him. Could I eventually end up loving him?

The possibility is there.

Do I believe he could fall in love with me?

I don't know, but the way he's acted toward me today leads me to believe anything is possible.

Anything.

Remaining in my dress and heels, I start to pack, quietly lamenting over the outfits and bikinis I didn't get to wear on this trip. I wonder if I have to return the unworn stuff when we get home.

My gut is telling me no.

I've just finished up with my packing and am

about to take a quick shower when there's a knock on the door. It swings open before I can say come in, and Perry is standing in the doorway, wearing a pair of black boxer briefs and nothing else.

"Hey."

I turn away from the suitcase on my bed to face him. "Hey. Everything okay?"

It takes all I've got to keep my focus on his face and not let my gaze drop to his boxers. Or his chest. Or whatever other naked part he's got on display.

"I have a question."

I frown. "What is it?"

He flicks his chin at me. "Whatcha got on under that dress?"

Hope lights up within me, and that familiar throb starts up between my thighs. "That's your question?"

"It's a valid one." He leans against the doorjamb, crossing his arms in front of his chest. "I realized I didn't want to spend the last night of our honeymoon without you, wife."

My heart pangs and I mentally tell it to calm down. "You're not so tired anymore?"

"Want me to be real with you?" I nod. "I'm exhausted."

"Oh."

"But come on." He tilts his head. "Sleep with me."

"Is that all you want?"

He stiffens, like I'm going to deny him. "Why do you ask?"

"Because." I approach him slowly, until I'm standing directly in front of him. "In answer to your original question, I have nothing on under this dress."

I brush past him before he can respond, heading down the hall toward his bedroom. He follows after me, picking up his steps, crowding me when I get to his bedroom door. I can feel him, hot and solid behind me and he reaches for the zipper at the back of my dress, slowly sliding it down.

"You need to get dressed for bed," he murmurs.

"You mean undressed?"

He chuckles. "Want to wear one of my T-shirts?"

I would love to, but only if he's worn it first. So it'll smell like him. But I can't admit that out loud, and besides, it would ruin the naked effect I was going for.

"I don't think so."

The zipper completely undone, he slides his

hands inside the dress, his fingers brushing against my sides. "We're taking this off?"

"You're taking it off." I tilt my head down when his hands sweep up to my shoulders, pushing the thin straps down my arms, until the entire dress falls to my feet. I kick it away, then slip out of my shoes. Until I'm completely naked and he's only in his boxer briefs and didn't he say something about sleeping together and that's it?

Stretching my arms above my head, I let loose an exaggerated yawn and make my way toward his bed. "I'm so tired."

He doesn't say a word. Just watches me like I've lost my mind, which maybe I have. My gaze drops to the front of his boxer briefs and I notice his cock. He doesn't have a full-blown erection, but it's getting there.

Once I'm under the covers and my head is resting on a pile of pillows, I pat the empty spot next to me. "Aren't you coming to bed?"

My question spurs him into action. He's turning off lights and closing the curtains, finally slipping beneath the covers, though he keeps his distance.

We're quiet. I can hear the sound of the ocean pounding the surf. That ever-present breeze softly rattling the palm trees.

"I'm going to miss this place," I admit.

"Yeah?"

"It's been peaceful."

"Not at first."

"That was more your fault than the location," I remind him.

"True." At least he doesn't deny it.

I glance over at him, taking in the outline of his face. "Thank you for bringing me here."

"You should be thanking my brother."

"I don't think you want me to thank him like I want to thank you," I say lightly.

Perry literally growls, grabbing hold of my arm and pulling me to him so I have no choice but to let him wrap me up in his strong arms. As if he's never going to let me go. He readjusts us so my back is to his front, my ass nudging his cock and he rests his chin on my shoulder, his mouth so close to my ear his lips tickle me when he speaks.

"I don't hate you anymore, wife."

I bend my head, shivering when he kisses my neck. "Are you so sure about that?"

His hands begin to wander, touching all of his favorite spots on my body. My breasts. My hips. My stomach. When he rests his hand on my pussy, I part my legs, allowing him entry, desperate for his fingers to work their magic.

"I'm positive," he whispers as he begins to slowly stroke me. "I told myself I wouldn't do this. That I was too tired. But I can't resist you."

When he rolls me over onto my back, I realize I can't resist him either.

He kisses me, and the foreign emotions rising within me are terrifying. Yet I chase after them anyway, seeking the high that only Perry can give me.

Chapter Eighteen

Perry

WINSTON CALLS ME into his office within ten minutes of my arrival at Halcyon. The moment I walk in, he's gesturing for me to close the door and I do so, falling into one of the chairs that's in front of his massive desk.

"How was the honeymoon?" he asks.

"Good." I don't need to go into detail. It's none of his damn business anyway, what happened between me and Charlotte.

"Just good? That's all you have to say?"

"You want me to tell you everything we did?" I raise my brows.

He seems amused. "If you're willing to do so. Go for it."

Irritation makes my blood hot. I'm still regretting we came home a day early, and I have no one to blame but myself.

"I'm not," I snap. "What did you want to talk about?"

Winston chuckles. "So sensitive."

I stare at him, annoyed.

"Let's talk about Seamus McTiernan." Winston reaches into his desk drawer and drops a thin file folder on top of his desk. "I have some information for you to read when you get a chance."

I stare at the folder, almost not wanting to open it. "We're going old school, huh? They can't send us the updates via email or text?"

"I put a guy on his tail that used to work for Dad." Winston's expression flashes with pain for the briefest moment. "He's got one of the best noses in the business."

"Nose?"

"He can sniff out any detail, no matter what. He might like to have his secretary type out his reports—who's his girlfriend, by the way, and he claims he can trust her like no one else to keep her mouth shut—but he uses every mode possible when on the hunt for his subject. The guy even knows how to use TikTok. And he's seventy," Winston says.

"It's the twenty-first century. I thought we were a little more sophisticated than this," I say.

"We have access to the best technology money can buy. This guy is better." My brother's firm tone is more like a taunt for me to argue with him.

I don't bother.

Leaning forward, I snatch the folder off of Winston's desk and flip it open. A black-and-white photo of Seamus McAsshole greets me, and I scowl when I recognize the building he's standing in front of.

"Where the Lancasters reside," Winston says for me. "He met with one of them."

Alarm races through me and I brace myself for the answer. I almost don't want to know. "Which one?"

"Not sure yet. Wasn't Grant. He was in his office—he's a workaholic like me. The youngest brother is away at boarding school. Louisa was in residence. So was Reggie."

I stare at the photo, wishing I could scratch Seamus's face out. "What about Finn?"

"Can't figure out where he is yet. He's mysterious, that one. Slippery too. Don't think he was the one who met with Seamus though," Winston says. "Pretty sure it was her dear old dad."

Anger rises and I do my best to tamp it down as I read through the report. The investigator gives a nearly hour-by-hour glimpse into this asshole's life for the last four days that we've been gone.

"He's been busy," I observe.

"I know. Meeting with various Morellis. A Lancaster. Surprised he didn't fit a meeting with a Constantine into his itinerary," Winston muses.

"What Constantine do you think he'd actually want to meet with?" I'd have a stern talk with *any* family member who spoke to this piece of shit.

"The only one I can imagine him wanting to meet with is your wife."

The anger blooms and I don't hold back. "He can go fuck himself. There's no way in hell I'll let him near her."

"You can't always protect her," Winston reminds me. "You're at work and she's at home and she'll eventually grow bored. She might even entertain the idea of reuniting with an old flame."

I slap the folder shut and drop it onto his desk with a plop. "Why are you trying to fuck with my head?"

"I'm not fucking with your head. I'm stating facts. And I'm hoping you'll agree with me when I say we can't trust her. Not yet."

The anger is automatically replaced with dread. "I don't trust her."

I'm a liar. I started to. The first part of the honeymoon, I was still pissed at the fact that her lover made a surprise appearance at our goddamn wedding. But as time went on and I spent more time with her, I realized that I actually *like* her. I'm definitely attracted to her. All that fucking in the hot Mexican sun does something to a person.

She told me how that asshole took advantage of her in Paris, and I trusted her with a story I've told no one else.

And that was a huge step for me. I don't like talking about my street racing days. Back then I did some things I regret.

I wish I wouldn't have shut her down when she was trying to open up to me. I was too selfish, too in my head to want to hear what she had to say when I should've remained quiet and listened.

Maybe she'll tell me again—and hopefully confess more.

"Good," Winston says, his expression grim. "For all we know she put Daddy up to meet with her ex and they're plotting to run away together with Daddy's permission."

That would never happen, is what I want to say. Her father is her worst nightmare. She wouldn't want to work with him.

"They don't get along," is all I say in response.

"Charlotte and her father."

"Uh-huh. She might get along with him for the sake of getting out of a marriage she never wanted," Winston points out.

"What else did this report say?" I ask, needing to change the subject.

Winston goes along with it, thank God. "He's not left the Morelli mansion for the last thirty-six hours. People are constantly coming and going out of that place, and Myron is still looking into who everyone is."

"Myron? That's our investigator's name?" I shake my head. "He even sounds old."

"He's a good guy. Gruff. Doesn't put up with anyone's shit. Even mine." Winston cracks a smile.

"You really think that McAsshole dude is plotting to somehow get to Charlotte?" I can't stop thinking about the possibility. How he might try to get close to her. Talk to her. What if she's receptive? What if he says all the right things? She chose that asshole first. I was merely assigned to her.

What if I lose her for good?

"You need to prepare for the possibility that it could happen. I recommend beefing up the security at your apartment."

"It's a Lancaster apartment," I remind him. "Daddy still has a key."

Winston frowns. "That's not good."

"I know."

"Change the locks. It's your and Charlotte's apartment now, right?"

"I don't have a deed or anything like that."

"Get one. Ask Charlotte to talk to her father."

I won't make her do that. She's frightened of him.

"If her father still has a key, he could give it to Seamus," I say, my mind awhirl with all of the possibilities. All of the awful, shitty, that-better-not-ever-happen possibilities.

Jesus.

"Like I said, beef up the security. Talk to your wife. Let her know what's going on. Don't leave her in the dark. She deserves to know her ex is a threat."

Says the guy who didn't tell the love of his life jack shit until it was almost too late.

"Learn from my mistakes," Winston continues, making me immediately regret my thoughts. "She's not your enemy, Perry. She's an ally, even if we don't necessarily trust her. Make her feel as if she's on team Constantine and she'll do whatever you ask her to do."

"She is a Constantine now, making her an automatic member of our team," I remind him.

"Not even a week ago she was a Lancaster. Remind her that she has a new allegiance. To you." Winston jabs a thumb at his chest. "To us."

I slouch in my chair, my mind crowded with too many things. All of them having to do with Charlotte and that jerk and the Morellis and her father.

Her father, a traitor to his own daughter—and to the family he just married her into. When he knew what he was getting into, making that deal with our mother. He was supposed to be team Constantine as well.

"I need to warn her." I start to get up but Winston speaks, halting me.

"Don't—scare her, little brother. Just make her aware that things aren't always what they seem. Maybe you shouldn't mention the meeting Seamus had with one of her family members yet."

"Why the hell not?"

"She might confront her father. Maybe her mother. For all we know, Louisa could be behind this."

I shake my head. "Doubtful. She only cares about shopping and going to lunch."

"Don't write her off like her husband does.

She's been married to that piece of shit for almost thirty years and she's still smiling. Hell, she's practically the queen of the Lancasters and he's only a second son," Winston reminds me.

I hate that I have that in common with my father-in-law—that we're both second sons in an important family. it's infuriating.

I don't want anything in common with him. I'd prefer to act like he doesn't even exist.

"Text your wife," Winston continues. "Check in with her throughout the day. Keep tabs on her."

"I never do that sort of thing." I grimace just thinking of it. I'm not a micromanaging control freak like my brother.

"Well, you're going to do it now. You need to know what your little bride is up to at all times. I'm assuming McTiernan used to have major sway over her. Who's to say he still doesn't?" Winston raises a brow, contemplating me.

While I sit and steam, wondering what the fuck kind of influence McDickface could still have on my wife. Not after she's been with me, is all I keep thinking.

But I might be wrong. Hell, she might still be in love with him.

I caught her texting someone a few times. Not

entirely sure I believe what she told me when I asked her about it either.

Was it him?

Just the thought of her texting that piece of shit she might still care about feels like a steel spike was rammed in my heart—and makes me want to rage.

CHAPTER NINETEEN

Charlotte

"MY KITTY MISSED me, didn't she?" I'm scratching Doja under her chin, smiling as she rubs her head against my hand. She's purring so loud I'm sure Jasper can hear her and he's in the kitchen while I'm in the living room.

Doja's golden gaze meets mine and she squints her eyes before she meows.

I'm guessing that was her answer.

Perry went back to work this morning and I miss him. I didn't wake up before he left like a good wife should, but our situation isn't normal, so I cut myself some slack. Besides, I was exhausted from the entire trip and I think it caught up to me. I feel bad about Perry having to go into work, but he wanted to. At least, that's what he told me last night, before we went to bed.

In separate rooms.

No sex to be had.

I missed him. I missed his touch and his scent and the commanding way he kisses me. I missed his heartbeat and his damp-with-sweat skin and his mouth at my ear, muttering filthy words.

A sigh leaves me and I squirm, making Doja meow as she hops off my lap.

Fickle girl.

"Would you like me to make you lunch?" Jasper asks as he strides into the living room.

I smile at him. I missed Jasper. Not because he does stuff for me or always wants to make me meals—which is not a normal job requirement for a butler, by the way. No, I missed him because the man listens to me. He offers sage advice. He even drops a sarcastic comment here and there, which I always appreciate.

I would love to talk to him about my marriage woes and ask if he knows what Perry might want in a wife, but I can't. Not yet. It still feels so private and new. And I don't want to break Perry's trust.

Knowing that he told me about the car racing when no one else that he's close to in his life does, made me feel special. As if he were giving me a little gift. A gift of his past.

I probably should've shared a story with him

as well, but what about? The up-and-down relationship with my father? How my mother neglects me most of the time? The age difference between my older brothers and me and how disconnected I feel to them sometimes. How much I miss Crew while he's away at Lancaster Prep, though I don't think he feels the same way about me?

My family is not one to discuss emotions. It's almost as if we don't have them. There weren't a lot of "love yous" shared by my parents growing up. Not a lot of encouragement either. Plenty of "You're a Lancaster. You can do it" type comments, but that was it.

No wonder I have issues. I cling to Perry's attention and soak it up like he might abandon me at any moment.

"Miss?" Jasper urges and I realize he's waiting for an answer.

Grabbing my phone, I check the time. "It's only ten thirty. I ate breakfast not even an hour ago."

"It wasn't much. You might grow hungry and want an early lunch." Jasper clasps his hands behind his back and studies me. "I must say your honeymoon left you with a lovely glow, miss." He frowns. "I probably shouldn't call you that, now that you're a married woman."

My Jasper is so proper. "Call me by my name."

He makes a face. "I couldn't. That's too—familiar."

"Jasper." I roll my eyes. "We've known each other a long time. I think it's okay if you call me Charlotte."

"Mrs. Constantine is what I should call you."

This immediately makes me think of Caroline. "And now I sound like my mother-in-law, when that is the last thing I want."

Jasper chuckles and my phone buzzes at the same time, indicating I got a text. I check who it's from.

Unknown number: *I miss you.*

My heart drops, and for a second, I think it might be my husband who said that.

I wish.

Me: *Who is this?*

Unknown number: *Think about it,* ***a runsearc****.*

My entire body goes cold at the endearment. I remember looking it up after he said it to me, and the literal meaning is secret love, which makes sense considering he didn't want anyone to know about us.

God, I was clueless. Young and naïve and just so stupid. I should've known then that it was a red flag.

> ***Me:*** *Stop texting me.*
>
> ***Unknown number:*** *I don't see how you can barely know a man yet marry him in a matter of weeks.*
>
> ***Me:*** *You don't know me anymore. I don't think you ever really did.*
>
> ***Unknown number:*** *I know you better than anyone. Especially that kid you consider your husband.*
>
> ***Me:*** *He IS my husband and he's not a kid.*
>
> ***Unknown number:*** *Compared to me he is.*

That's true. Seamus is in his thirties. He probably has a solid ten years on Perry.

What was I doing, falling for Seamus's lies when I was in Paris? So starved for affection I gave it up to the first man who showed me attention. A much older man with a prestigious position and a beautiful girlfriend who wanted to be his wife.

I was a complete idiot.

"I'm going to prepare you a nice salad," Jasper says, making me glance up from my phone. "I'll put it in the refrigerator when I'm done and you can eat it whenever you're ready. Just let me know."

I frown at him. "Are you bored, Jasper? Not much to do around here for you?"

"No, I'm not bored." He shakes his head, but I can tell he's fibbing. "Would you care to see what I've trained Doja to do?"

Whatever distraction he can give me to forget about Seamus, I need it. "Please. I would love to."

"You won't get mad?"

"Why would I get mad?"

Doja follows Jasper everywhere he goes. He's like her second owner. Plus, he feeds her more often than I do, which is always a draw for her. Her love and loyalty are led by her stomach. "She is your cat."

"And she's yours too. She adores you. Look at her." My phone buzzes over and over with texts from Seamus but I ignore him. To give in gives him exactly what he wants.

My attention.

"Very well, then. I'll show you." Jasper disappears, Doja trotting after him and I pick up my phone with dread, checking my messages. They're not all from Seamus, though most of them are.

Unknown number: *You can't ignore me*

forever. We should get together soon. I would love to catch up.

Unknown number: *Don't you ever think of me? Remember the good times we shared? There were plenty. Not everything was bad between us, Charlotte. Once upon a time, I do think you loved me.*

I didn't know what love was—I still don't. It was a silly infatuation that bloomed into a full-blown affair that cost me the rest of my semester in Paris.

Only because I ran away like a child, but at the time, I still was one.

Me: *There's nothing for us to catch up on. I don't want to see you, Seamus. Please leave me alone.*

Unknown number: *Tell me you love him and I will.*

I don't bother answering him. I block his number instead, then check my other text.

One from my husband.

Perry: *I have a surprise for you.*

My stomach flutters with excitement at that one simple sentence.

If I don't watch it, I could completely and

totally fall for this man. And I don't mind the idea of it one bit.

Me: *What is it?*

Perry: *If I told you, it wouldn't be a surprise.*

Me: *Then why are you even bringing it up?*

Perry: *Because I need your cooperation. I want you to be ready for me at seven o'clock. I'll pick you up in front of the building.*

Seven is so far away. An eternity. I don't know how I'll wait that long.

Me: *How should I dress?*

Perry: *What do you mean?*

Me: *Oh come on, my fashionable husband. What sort of outfit should I wear? Casual? Dressy?*

Perry: *Panties or no panties?*

My entire body flushes hot.

Me: *Yes, all of that. These are important details I need to know before you pick me up.*

Perry: *Dress casual. Panties optional.*

I'm full-blown giddy now. All texts from Seamus completely pushed out of my mind.

Me: *I'm intrigued.*

Perry: *You should be, wife.*

I like it when he calls me wife.

And I'm definitely not wearing panties for this so-called casual excursion. I have no idea where he might be taking me, but I know I'll enjoy the ride.

Chapter Twenty

Perry

THE MOMENT I'M in the driver's seat of the Chevelle, I exhale on a sigh of total relief.

It feels like coming home.

Which is some corny-ass shit, I'm not gonna lie. But damn, it's been a long time since I've been behind the wheel of my orange baby, and it feels fucking good.

Like I'm on top of the world.

I shove the key in the ignition and crank it, pleased that it easily starts with a low rumble. I found a mobile car mechanic who met me at the garage and tinkered around under the hood, making sure it was at full running capacity. The battery needed a jump thanks to it sitting for so long, but otherwise he declared it ready to use.

"That is one fine-looking vehicle," he told me just before he left, his gaze appreciative as he stared at my precious Chevelle. "You could command a pretty penny for it if you decided to ever sell it."

"Never," I said vehemently. "This is my most prized possession."

Leaning forward, I run my hand along the smooth dashboard. Fiddle with the knobs on the radio until classic rock blares from the speakers. It seemed fitting, to listen to a little Led Zeppelin while driving this baby uptown to our apartment.

Led Zeppelin was one of my father's favorite bands. Didn't quite go with the suit-and-tie, boardroom behavior my father always lived by, but that's what I loved about him. He wasn't just one thing; he was multi-faceted.

I hope people consider me in the same light.

Ignoring the fear that's suddenly coursing through my blood, I put the vehicle in reverse and back it out of the parking spot, the wheels squealing. I wasn't even going that fast.

Okay. I'm lying. I always go fast in this baby.

As I drive to our apartment, I get a few honks of appreciation. Not every day you see a classic set of wheels driving in the middle of Manhattan. My family all hate this damn car, and at one point, after the accident, I did too.

But how could I hate this beauty? She gives

me nothing but pure pleasure, and once I get my wife in the passenger seat and take her on a joy ride, forget it.

It's going to feel so damn good seeing Charlotte sitting next to me, smiling and laughing as I drive too fast on the city streets, I just might fucking explode with happiness.

My mind goes back to what Winston told me earlier. I've already put a plan into action. Security was called and we'll have a couple of extra guards patrolling the building or standing watch by our door in a day or two. I called a locksmith and he'll be out tomorrow to change out the locks. Had to pay him extra to get him there in less than twenty-four hours but my peace of mind is worth it.

That and my wife's safety. The most important thing of all. You'd think her own damn father would agree and do his best to try and protect her.

Fucker. He could give two shits about his own daughter.

Anger grips me and I curl my fingers around the steering wheel so tight, I'm white-knuckling it, telling myself I can't let what Winston revealed ruin my night. I've had this planned since the flight home yesterday. I knew after I told

Charlotte about my near-death experience in the Chevelle that I wanted to take her for a ride in the car. I don't want to scare her—and I get the feeling my daredevil side most definitely scares her—but I want to show her this part of me. How I used to race, and I was damn good at it.

That's something I don't want to involve myself in anymore but I'm perfectly willing to drive this baby around the city and have a good time. We could grab some dinner. Maybe drive up to Bishop's Landing and I can show her where I grew up. Then head back home, get naked and fuck each other's brains out.

Yeah. That sounds like the perfect night.

The moment I pull up in front of the building, I'm grabbing my phone, about to text Charlotte when the building door opens and she's there, heading straight for the car, her mouth dropping open in shock. I'd roll down the passenger window to say something to her but it's got a crank handle, so I just wait for her to open the door.

Within seconds she does exactly that, ducking her head so she can study me. "Perry!"

I grin. I can't help it. "What do you think?"

"It's…" She bursts out laughing as she stands up straight and stares at my precious baby. "It's super orange."

"That's my favorite part." Not really. The engine is what makes my dick hard.

Not that my car actually makes my dick hard...

"It's beautiful." She ducks her head back inside and I want to tell her she's the beautiful one. I don't think I've ever seen her look so pretty. Her eyes are sparkling and her hair is down and perfectly straight. She has on a flower-print dress with a denim jacket over it, and while I figured she'd show up in jeans and a sweater, this casual look works for me too.

"Get in," I demand and she does as I ask, settling her sweet self into the passenger seat, her gaze roaming the interior, as if she doesn't know where to look first. "What do you think?"

"It's really nice. It looks brand new."

"She's in pristine condition." I smooth my hand over the dash yet again. Like I get off on stroking this car. Seriously, I'm nuts.

"What year?"

"1969, baby." I grin at her when she slams her door shut. "Wine me, dine me, sixty-nine me."

Charlotte wrinkles her nose. "No one has ever done that to me."

"Wined you and dined you?"

"Sixty-nined me." Her cheeks turn pink.

My mind immediately goes to Charlotte on top of me, her pussy and ass right in my face, her mouth wrapped around my dick. "We're going to have to try that sometime."

"Have you ever done that before? Oh my God, don't answer that question. I don't want to know." She shakes her head vehemently.

We never talk about my previous sexual experiences because they weren't that memorable. As in, I never had a lasting relationship beyond a couple of casual hookups with the same person. "Want me to be real with you right now?"

"Probably not."

I ignore her answer. "I've never done it."

She's quiet for a moment, her head slowly swiveling in my direction so she can stare at me. "Really?"

I nod. "Seemed like a lot of work." And rather intimate.

Wouldn't mind being rather intimate with my wife, though.

"Still not interested, then?"

"Didn't have it on the agenda tonight, but things can change." I shift the car into first gear and leave my foot on the clutch. "Ready to go?"

"Where are you taking me?"

"On the ride of your life," I answer without hesitation.

Her smile is huge and the sound of her laughter…

Fuck. It just does something to me.

"Let's go," she says eagerly.

I glance in the side mirror, the road clearing just in time for me to ease up on the clutch and pull onto the street, the tires loud, the engine louder.

But they've got nothing on the sound of my wife's laugh.

I go fast and take corners faster, making her squeal in delight. In horror. She can't stop laughing and I figure it's some sort of nervous thing too, because her expression is equal parts joy and terror.

Eventually I slow down, feeling bad that I'm frightening her. She seems to relax, her body melting into the seat.

"You hungry?"

"Kind of." She blows out a shaky breath. "You're a little scary."

"I was actually taking it easy compared to how I used to drive this thing."

I can feel her staring at me like I'm a complete stranger. "That was taking it easy? I can't imagine what you must've been like when you were racing."

"An absolute terror." I say it proudly.

Her laughter is back, and it's real this time. "There is so much more to you than I even know."

"You have no idea, wife. We've barely scratched the surface." I glance over at her to see she's smiling, staring out the passenger side window and looking very pleased with herself. I reach over, pushing up the hem of her skirt so I can rest my hand on her bare knee. "You take my 'panties optional' rule to heart?"

She keeps her gaze on the window. "Maybe you should look and see."

I slide my fingers up the inside of her slender thigh, silently marveling at her soft skin. She parts her legs slightly, giving me better access and soon enough I'm encountering nothing but bare, creamy heat.

"No panties," she murmurs, her hot gaze meeting mine as I lightly stroke her.

"Is that why you wore a dress?" I brush her clit with my thumb.

She bites her lower lip, nodding. "You like?"

Is it wrong that it makes my dick hard that I'm fingering my wife in my favorite car? Probably not.

"I fucking love," I answer, steering the car with one hand to the right so I can eventually park along the curb. I haven't been paying attention to where we're at. Just driving aimlessly around Manhattan and I realize we're in a quiet residential neighborhood. Reluctantly I remove my hand from my wife and downshift. "Think anyone would give a shit if I got you off in front of their brownstone?"

Charlotte glances over at the row of homes I'm currently parking in front of. I put the car into park. "Spread your legs wider, baby."

She does as I ask without hesitation, knowing I'll deliver. My hand is back under her dress and I slide two fingers into her tight channel. I start thrusting, nice and slow, my gaze trained on her the entire time. The myriad emotions I see streaking across her face. The way she opens and closes her mouth when I stroke her extra hard. The little gasps. The whimpers, her eyelids fluttering as she struggles to keep them open.

Unable to stand it any longer, I lean over and kiss her. Consume her. I thrust my tongue into her mouth and do a thorough sweep before I twist my tongue around hers, her whimpers coming faster now. Her hips move with my hand and she's so wet, my fingers slick through her noisily, the only other sound our accelerated breaths.

"Perry," she whispers against my lips, her entire body growing stiff. "I missed you."

"I missed you too," I tell her, shoving three fingers inside her, my thumb pressing against her clit at the same time, rubbing it in small, tight circles.

"Oh God," she chokes out, her inner walls clenching around my fingers just before she starts to shake. "*Perrrrrrry.*"

I kiss her hard to shut her up. I don't need her yelling my name and disturbing the neighborhood, though that would be kind of hot.

That's my wife. She's sexy as fuck and so damn responsive. I didn't mean to take it this far this fast tonight, but damn it, I *do* plan on fucking her in this car sometime. Preferably after we eat dinner.

I'm fucking starving.

She moans into my mouth and it's the sexiest sound. I ease my speed, until eventually I pull my fingers out of her completely, breaking the kiss to push my fingers into her mouth. She sucks them eagerly, her hot tongue licking, my dick surging against the fly of my jeans I changed into before I left the office.

I did not want to drive this car in a suit. Talk about a mismatch.

"What are you doing to me?" she asks when I withdraw my now clean fingers from her mouth.

I study her. Her eyes are glazed and her cheeks are flushed and her lips are swollen. She looks wiped out. In a daze.

All thanks to me.

"I'd like to know what the fuck you're doing to me." I lean in and drop a kiss on her lips, lingering there. And I'm not talking just sexually either.

What exactly is going on between us? This isn't like the business deal we first started with, that's for damn sure. What is she doing when I'm not around? If she's playing my ass, I'm going to feel like the biggest fool out there. I don't think I could survive the humiliation.

My family alone will make me feel like a giant loser. I don't need the rest of the world chiming in with their opinions about my marriage to Charlotte Lancaster.

"I used to read witchcraft books," she tells me, a new tidbit she's never shared before. "Maybe I cast a spell on you."

"I think it worked." I kiss her again before she can tell me more. "I think I like you, wife."

"I know I like you," she admits, biting her

lower lip. I must give her a questioning look because she continues on. “What? I do.”

“You’re loyal to me? To the Constantines?” I lift a brow, waiting for her answer. Hating how heavy my chest suddenly feels.

“What else do I need to do.” She leans in closer to me, her face practically in mine. “To prove that I would never want to hurt you?”

I stare into her blue eyes, pleased by her words, and the meaning behind them. “I don’t want to hurt you either.”

Her smile is faint. “Good. We’re on the same page, then.”

“Let’s go to a diner for dinner.” My stomach hurts, I’m so hungry. And she doesn’t even bat an eyelash at my change of subject.

“What? And eat greasy hamburgers and French fries coated in salt?” Her brows lift.

Nodding, I kiss her again. Like I can’t get enough. “Sounds fucking delicious.”

“Okay,” she whispers.

“And after we eat, I’ll take you somewhere with a nice view and fuck you nice and slow in the back seat of the car?”

“I’d rather fuck you in the front seat, with it pushed all the way back,” she suggests softly.

I smile.

“Deal.”

CHAPTER TWENTY-ONE

Charlotte

IT FEELS LIKE Perry and I are on a real date, which is kind of funny because it means we've been doing this relationship thing completely backwards. Not that I mind.

Well, I did mind, but I learned how to work with it and now I actually like Perry.

I especially like Perry when he drives fast, with that easy confidence behind the wheel, despite how much it scared me. He looked so relaxed, his body slouched, one hand on the wheel, the wind blowing through his hair after he rolled the window down.

And I really like it when he reaches over and slips his fingers between my thighs. That was all sorts of hot. I didn't mean to come so fast but I wasn't lying when I told him I missed him.

That I was horny for him.

All damn day.

We're at a diner I found thanks to me searching on Google. It had good reviews and it looked crowded when we pulled into the parking lot—all good signs. The moment we got seated, we both ordered cheeseburgers and fries plus two milkshakes. I got strawberry and he got chocolate.

"What made you get the Chevelle out?" I ask him after our milkshakes are delivered and we're spooning up ice cream and shoveling it into our mouths like a couple of little kids.

"Telling you about racing made me miss her." He licks his spoon, the sight of his tongue doing things to me. Twisting me up inside.

Making me want him.

"She's a her, huh?"

He nods, dunking his spoon back into his milkshake and swirling it around. They served the milkshakes to us in those old-fashioned green glasses, the spoon handles skinny and long so they can reach the bottom. "Never actually named her though."

"You should," I suggest, trying to slow down from eating too much ice cream. I still have a cheeseburger and fries to enjoy. "What girl names do you like?"

"Charlotte." He grins, a thin line of chocolate

sitting on his upper lip. "That name is cute."

"Too formal." I tap my upper lip. "You've got—"

"Thanks." He grabs a napkin and cleans his face. "You don't like your name?"

I shake my head. "I always wanted an 'ee' name."

He frowns. "What do you mean?"

"Rylie. Kylie. Mylie. Kaylee. Hailey. All my friends in school had names like that. Even my cousin Sylvie. And here I was with a total clunker of a name. Charlotte." I make a face and shake my head, giving in and shoving a big scoop of strawberry ice cream into my mouth.

"I like Charlotte," he says and I'm sure he's just saying that to make me feel better, though I don't say that out loud. "I have an 'ee' name as you call it. And I hate it."

"You want me to be truthful with you?"

He nods, his expression turning serious. "Always."

"When I first saw your name, I thought you were an old man."

He leans back against the bright red booth seat, shaking his head. "It's the worst. Who the hell else do you know my age named Perry?"

"It makes you stand out."

"It sucks."

"Why were you named Perry? Do you know?"

"Old family name, I guess. That's what I've been told at least." He swirls his spoon in the ice cream, pulling it out to lick it again.

He needs to stop doing that. He's making me squirm.

"Why were you named Charlotte?" he asks me when I still haven't said anything.

"Old family name," I repeat with a faint smile. "There are a couple of Charlotte Lancasters out there that predate me."

"You talk to your parents lately?" he asks, seemingly out of the blue.

I study him, wondering what he's getting at. But his expression is completely neutral and he keeps licking at his spoon which is a distraction. "No. Not really."

"What do you mean, not really?" His voice is casual, but there was a sharp gleam in his eye for a moment.

Now it's gone.

"My mother called earlier today to make sure I made it back okay. I told her I did. Then I had to go because Jasper was showing me what he taught Doja to do."

Perry frowns. "What did he teach her?"

"How to fetch! It's the cutest thing. He balls up a piece of paper and throws it, and she goes and gets it and brings it back to him! I tried it with her but she kept bringing the paper ball to Jasper instead."

I laugh just thinking about it. We played fetch with her for at least an hour, maybe longer.

"Sounds fun." He smiles, tilting his head back when the server stops by our table and sets our plates in front of us.

"Here you go, kids," the older woman says, snapping her gum. "You need anything else? More water? Maybe a Coca-Cola?"

"I'll take more water," I say as Perry leans over for the ketchup and plucks the bottle from where it sits, cracking open the lid and dumping a bunch onto his plate.

"I'm good," Perry tells her.

"Be right back." She smiles at us before she takes off.

"This place feels straight out of a movie," I tell him when she's gone. It's all kitschy red and white diner décor with Coca-Cola signs everywhere, mixed with a couple of cool neon signs. There are rows of vintage records pinned up on the top of the walls and the floors are black and white checkerboard.

"It's cool, right?" Perry picks up his burger and takes a giant bite, groaning as he starts to chew. "This is fucking delicious."

I grab my burger with both hands—it's huge—and bite into it, moaning in pleasure as soon as it hits my taste buds. "Oh, this is *so* good."

"Right?" He keeps taking bites, like he can't stop.

"How was work?" I ask after I set my burger down and grab the ketchup, adding some to my plate before I drag a couple of fries through it. They're crispy, hot, and delicious.

"Long day."

That's all he offers.

"How's your brother?"

"Grumpy." He takes another bite.

Again, that's all he says.

Why is he not telling me much? I don't even know what he does for Halcyon. Something about customer care? No, that doesn't sound quite right. Winston is the grumpy CEO who makes demands and Perry is the one who sweeps in afterward and sweetens the deal with his endearing personality and charm.

My husband, the sweetheart.

Though he can be ferocious. Moody and gray.

Mean and restless.

"Are you grumpy too?" I ask after a few minutes of silence while we eat.

He lifts his gaze to mine. "I'm not grumpy. I just—don't want to talk about work. It's boring."

"You don't like your job?"

"I love it." His smile feels downright false. "I'd just rather focus on other things. Like how Jasper supposedly trained your cat to fetch."

"There's no supposedly about it. He totally trained her. I'll have to show you when we get home, though she'll probably be snoozing."

"Catch it on video and send it to me," he suggests, his phone dinging right on cue. He checks it, frowning slightly before he shoves his phone back into his jeans pocket. "You having fun?"

His question catches me off guard and I smile at him, touched that he asked. "Yes. This is the best date I've ever been on."

"You must not have dated much."

"Not at all."

His gaze is assessing. "You don't even want to know what I'm thinking right now."

I know what he's thinking about, because I'm thinking about him too. Is Seamus always going to pop up between us like this?

God, I hope not.

✧ ✧ ✧

WE EXIT THE diner to discover it started raining and I yank my denim jacket over my head, running to the car, following after Perry, who unlocks the door and opens it for me so I can slip inside. The moment he's in the driver's seat, he revs the engine and zooms off, his face full of intense concentration as he drives the wet city streets. I try not to let myself get too caught up in him, but it's no use.

I'm completely caught up in him. The sexy way he drives, the expression on his handsome face, the way he stays focused, though I'm sure he feels me watching him.

It's like I can't stop watching him.

"Where are we going?" I ask at one point and he just shakes his head, his lips curved into a closed-mouth smile.

"You'll see."

He eventually pulls into a parking garage at Battery Park, driving until we're all the way on the top level. He pulls the car into a spot facing the water, putting it into gear and cutting the engine. We sit in silence for a moment, the ticking of the cooling engine the only sound and finally I can't take it anymore.

I steal a glance at him to find he's already watching me, all that intensity he had driving now focused entirely on me. I lean back a little bit, sucking in a breath and he slowly shakes his head.

"Don't look scared, wife."

"Can we see the water from here?" I turn my attention to the windshield, sitting up a little bit in my seat, but I can't see beyond the concrete half wall in front of us.

"You really want to check out the views right now? Or the back seat?"

My skin tingles at the promise in his voice. "I thought we were going to do it in the front seat."

"It'll be tight."

My gaze returns to his. "I like it tight," I whisper.

He's on me in seconds, his hands in my hair, his mouth finding mine. The kiss is sloppy and dirty, his tongue thrusting, low groans sounding in his chest. As if he can't get enough of me.

I feel the same. The exact same.

He undoes my seat belt and I go to him, climbing on top of his lap, my butt nudging the steering wheel and honking the horn. I startle and start to laugh, as does he, his hands curling around my face and pulling me down for another kiss.

Oh God, this feels too real right now. To real and too *right.* I love how he's touching me. His hands slide from my face to my neck. Down my front to curl around my breasts. He squeezes and kneads them, my nipples beading beneath his palms and I thrust my chest into his hands, needing more.

"Think we'll get caught?" I whisper to him when his hands drop to my thighs, gathering up the fabric of my skirt.

"Isn't that half the fun?" He smirks, yanking the fabric up before his hands dive beneath. "Rise up."

I do as he says, a jolt running through me when his seeking fingers find my wet pussy. He strokes and teases. Circles and presses until I'm a moaning mess, my back pressed against the solid weight of the steering wheel. It hurts.

I don't care.

"You sure you don't want the back seat?" he asks yet again and I hurriedly shake my head, reaching for the front of his jeans. I undo the buttons, curling my fingers around his cotton-covered cock and he surges in my hand.

Always ready for me.

Somehow we fumble with our clothing and

his jeans and boxer briefs end up bunched around his calves and my denim jacket ends up on the floorboard. I've got my dress gathered up in one hand as I carefully lower myself onto his thick cock, taking him in inch by inch.

By the time he's filling me completely, we're both moaning, our mouths finding each other's in a savage kiss.

We move as one, the interior of the car growing muggy from our heated skin. Our ragged breaths. The rain increases in tempo, matching our pace and my clit throbs every time I thrust down. He didn't put on a condom and I don't even care.

I want to feel him come inside me. Mark me.

Claim me as his.

"Charlotte," he whispers, his hands coming to my face again, his fingers streaking across my cheeks. I open my eyes to find him watching me, his lips parted, his chest rising and falling rapidly. He's so deeply embedded inside of me it's as if we're fused together.

Like we belong to each other.

He doesn't say anything else. Just my name. I bend my head, pressing my forehead to his, staring into his eyes as I work my hips, riding him hard, desperate to consume him. I close my eyes when he kisses me, his teeth nipping, tongue licking.

It's so good between us. Too good. Natural and perfect and delicious. I never want him to stop fucking me.

Ever.

Perry rests his hands on my hips, rendering me still as he thrusts and thrusts, his cock filling me again and again until a keening cry sounds and I clutch him to me, the orgasm washing over me with an intensity that leaves me breathless. Boneless.

"Jesus," he mutters, his mouth on my neck as he groans into my skin. His shoulders tense beneath my grip and then he's coming too. His semen floods me like a hot blast and I clench all around him, trying to keep it inside.

Like...what? I want something to take so I can get pregnant? I don't think so.

But would it be so bad, having Perry's baby? He'd be a blond-haired, blue-eyed little charmer. Adorable as can be. I'm sure our mothers would be positively thrilled. They didn't expect us to even get along, let alone procreate and have babies.

I run my hands through Perry's hair, making it wilder than it already is. He's got his face buried against the front of my neck, his hot breath blowing across my skin, making me shiver. He's still inside of me but I can feel him softening.

"We should go," I whisper.

"Don't go." His arms tighten around me, locking me in place. "I'm having a moment."

"What do you mean?"

He slowly tilts his head back, his heavy gaze finding mine. "I fucked my girl in the front seat of my favorite car. Best night ever."

I laugh.

I kiss him.

I can't even begin to describe what I'm feeling for this man right now.

Chapter Twenty-Two

Perry

"I HAD A thought," I say as I stroll into Winston's office, my hands in my pockets, my mood disgustingly cheerful.

Meaning it's even disgusting to me, how damn cheerful I am.

Winston holds up a finger, his phone glued to his ear as he listens to whatever he's being told. "Right," he says when the person on the other end finishes speaking. "And I'm telling you I don't give a fuck. Find out what's going on. Now."

He ends the call and slams his phone onto his desk, immediately checking the screen to make sure he didn't crack it, which sort of ruins the entire violent effect he was going for.

But whatever. It's not bugging me. This is what happens when you have sex in your car and then take your wife home and fuck her in your bed too. I didn't get a good night's sleep but it doesn't matter. I'm sated. Satisfied.

While my big brother is tense and grouchy as fuck. Great.

"I had a couple of text messages come through right before the wedding. I don't know who they came from, but they were rude as hell. They were about Charlotte," I tell him.

Winston rolls his eyes. "A couple of rude texts about your new wife and you're only just now telling me about them? When they happened a few weeks ago?"

"I forgot about them. I've been a little busy." I shrug. I didn't necessarily think they were a threat, but now…

I don't know. They make me uneasy.

"Let me see them." Winston flicks his fingers at me in a grabby motion and I bring them up on my phone before I hand it over. He snatches the phone from me and reads them, his brows lowered.

"The number is blocked," Winston says.

No shit, is how I want to answer him but I restrain myself.

"I know."

Winston squints, reading them again. "It says 'nothing a fat dick in her mouth won't fix.' You think it's from her ex?"

"Maybe. I didn't think anything of it when I got them. Then I was caught up in wedding shit and forgot." As I lay in bed last night with my wife tucked up all around me, naked and warm and with her hair in my face, I remembered them.

And I didn't like them. At all. Now that I know McAsswipe is up to no fucking good, I'm starting to wonder if he's the one who sent them to me.

That's so obvious though. Not very Morelli of him at all—they're a hell of a lot sneakier.

Most of the time.

"You should've told me about these a long time ago." Winston hands over my phone and I take it from him. "I'm having Myron look into your phone records. The incoming and outgoing calls, all of them. That won't be an issue, will it?"

"Why would it be?" I raise my brows.

"In case you've got any secrets you don't want getting out." His tone is casual, though the look on his face is anything but.

"If you're trying to imply I'm up to no good and doing something I don't want you to know, you have nothing to worry about," I say dryly. "I have no secrets."

"Good." Winston seems pleased. "I always

have to mention it. I don't know if you're seeing another woman right now."

"I am definitely not seeing another woman." I hold up my left hand, flashing him the ring my wife gave me. "I'm married."

"That doesn't mean shit and you know it, Perry. Especially between you two," Winston mutters.

"You cheating on Ash?" I throw at him.

He seems taken aback. Just before he switches to furiously angry. "What the fuck? How dare you—"

"See, it sucks, saying that kind of shit. Of course you wouldn't cheat on her. I wouldn't cheat on Charlotte," I say, flopping into the chair that sits across from Winston's desk. I feel like we're on a repeat of yesterday.

"Your marriage isn't based on—love." Winston spits out the last word, like he has a difficult time saying it.

"I care about her though." I think of her climbing on top of me last night. The way she slid onto my dick, riding me in the driver's seat of the Chevelle. Hot as fuck. Every fantasy come to life, right there in that moment.

"You're just excited because you're getting free pussy every night without having to ask for it,"

Winston mutters.

"Don't talk about my wife like that," I snap.

His gaze dances as he contemplates me, swiveling in his desk chair. "Oh so defensive. Even more than you were yesterday."

I rise to my feet, irritated. "Look into those text messages. See what Myron comes up with."

"Will do, little brother. I'll keep you posted. Oh, and I'll run a search on your wife's phone records too. Brace yourself though."

I pause at his office door, glancing over my shoulder. "Why?"

"Might find out something you don't want to know."

I leave his office, marching toward my own and throwing myself into my desk chair, staring unseeingly at my dark computer screen. I hate how unsettled my brother's words make me feel. He still doesn't trust Charlotte and I get why. He doesn't know her. Doesn't have to deal with her daily and see her smiling face and sparkling blue eyes. The way she says my name when I'm buried inside her to the hilt, making her come.

Yeah, he doesn't know. He doesn't have a fucking clue.

I grab my phone and send her a quick text to check on her.

> **Me:** *What are you doing?*

She doesn't immediately respond and that fills me with alarm. Maybe she's busy. In the shower. Chatting with Jasper—those two are close. He's like her second dad or something. She mentioned she might try and call her little brother this afternoon and I told her she should invite him to our place for the weekend. I want to get to know him.

The happiness on her face when I made that suggestion is hard to describe. How could a woman who looks like that at me be up to no good? Sneaking around on me on the side?

Nope. I don't believe it. She's loyal to me. She said so herself last night.

That woman is mine.

My phone buzzes and I immediately check it.

> **Charlotte:** *Training Doja. I threw the ball and she brought it back to me instead of Jasper! This is major.*

I smile. I wonder if that's what she wants to do with the rest of her days. Train her cat? Hang out with her friend the butler? That doesn't sound like much. Does she have dreams and aspirations? And am I the piece-of-shit, not-interested husband who never asked her about them?

I should. Tonight, at dinner I'm going to question her. Drive her out of her mind with my curiosity. All I want is for her to be happy. Fulfilled.

Me: *You take a video of it so I can see?*

Charlotte: *I forgot! I will next time she does it. I'll give my phone to Jasper.*

Me: *Thanks for the warning. I'll hold off sending the dick pic I was planning for now.*

I send her a string of eggplant emojis as a substitute.

She goes quiet and I set my phone on my desk, chuckling to myself as I turn to face the window, staring at the city spread out before me. Haven't heard from my mother yet, which is odd. I'm surprised she hasn't reached out to me since we returned home, eager to have dinner with my blushing bride so she can show us all the housing options she found in Bishop's Landing for us.

I don't want to move there. I'm over it. I want to stay right where we're at and enjoy our time in the city. We can live in Bishop's Landing later, when we have a kid or two and we're not wanting to raise them in the big city.

Damn, I sound whipped as fuck. And I don't even mind.

Another text comes through and I see it's a video from Charlotte of Doja the cat doing exactly as she described. Charlotte throws the balled-up piece of paper and the cat bolts off like a shot, grabbing the ball in her teeth and trotting back over to where Charlotte waits, dropping the ball onto her feet.

Charlotte squeals, grabbing the cat and giving her a big squeeze, Doja meowing and trying to scramble out of her arms.

I receive a text from my wife too.

Charlotte: *OMG I'm so glad you didn't send a dick pic when Jasper was filming. Talk about embarrassing.*

Me: *Your cat is tricky.*

Charlotte: *Isn't she great? I think I'm going to put her in movies. Cats are so hard to train!*

I don't bother arguing with her. I'm sure the majority of them are easy to train, but what the hell do I know about cats?

Me: *You still want that dick pic?*

Charlotte: *I never said I wanted it.*

Me: *But do you?*

Charlotte: *Perry.*

I check to make sure my office door is shut

before I'm undoing my belt and unzipping my pants, my cock out in seconds. It's semi-hard and I give it a couple of strokes, thinking of Charlotte kneeling before me in the office, her lips wrapped around just the tip.

We need to recreate that fantasy, stat.

When I'm erect enough for my satisfaction, I grab my phone and take a photo, then ponder if I should send it or not.

Fuck it.

I hit send and wait. She doesn't disappoint.

My phone rings within seconds.

"Perry," is all she says when I answer the phone and the scandalous tone of her voice is enough to make me burst out laughing. "I can't believe you sent that!"

"Did Jasper see?"

"No!" she shrieks. "But he was in the room with me."

I chuckle. "Then you're safe."

"Doja saw."

"Was she impressed?"

"She's a cat. Nothing impresses her." Charlotte lowers her voice. "What are you doing in your office with a hard-on?"

"Thinking about my wife." My voice is low too, my heart thudding hard against my chest. It's true. That's all it takes.

I think of her and I'm instantly aroused.

She's quiet for a moment. "You're naughty."

"Tell me you're not turned on."

"I can't tell you that because it would be a lie."

I am smug as fuck. "That's what I thought."

"You should come home early tonight."

"Why? You got something special planned for dinner?"

Ah the little woman, fixing me a home-cooked meal. That's a total fantasy I don't think is ever going to actually happen, but a man can dream.

"Yeah, I do." Her voice drops to the softest whisper. "Me."

I sit up straight, tucking my dick back into my underwear, which is awkward as fuck considering I still have a boner. "I'll leave now."

She laughs. "Give me some time first! Leave in an hour and we have a deal."

"Will do."

I end the call and lean back in my chair, not caring if my zipper is still undone and I've got a delirious grin plastered on my face. Anyone could walk in, even my mother, and I wouldn't give a single fuck. I am feeling too good.

For once, everything seems to be going right. Smoothly.

Almost feels too good to be true.

CHAPTER TWENTY-THREE

Charlotte

"MISS." I GLANCE up from the book I'm reading on my phone to find Jasper standing in front of me, a concerned expression on his face. "Someone, er, wants to speak with you."

I frown, glancing at the time on my phone. It's almost three. No one asks to speak to me here ever. "Who is it?"

"He—wouldn't say. I was informed that he's an old friend and you would understand when I told you he was from Paris."

I leap off the couch, my phone falling from my lap to the floor. "Where is he? You didn't let him into the apartment, did you?"

Jasper shakes his head. "I told him I needed to speak with you first."

"And how exactly did you speak with him?"

Panic grips me around the throat and I glance around the cavernous living room. The only other living thing I see is my cat.

"The man working the security desk called and wanted me to relay the message. What would you like me to tell him?"

Curiosity eats at me and I rest my hands on my hips, contemplating my options. I could ignore Seamus and he'll keep coming around, making a nuisance of himself. Or I could go down to the lobby in front of all sorts of people—including security—in the middle of the afternoon and tell him once and for all that I'm not interested.

Ever.

I'm a married woman. And I care about my husband. I'm Perry's wife, and he's the only one who matters in my life.

I'm certainly not going to cheat on him with Seamus.

I look at that relationship now for what it was. A crush that turned into something real, only for it to be built on nothing but lies. I was devastated, I was hurt, but I got over it.

Yes. I am completely over it.

"I'll go down and meet with him," I announce.

Jasper frowns. Doja meows in seeming protest—her timing is always impeccable. "I don't know if that's a good idea."

"There will be all sorts of people down there, right? Doormen and security and that one woman who sits at the front counter sometimes," I tell Jasper.

He tilts his head to the side, imagining the scene, I assume. "Well, I suppose."

"And it'll only be a few minutes. What I have to say to him won't take long. You'll know where I'm at."

"Should I go down with you?"

I shake my head. I won't be able to act like a badass bitch in front of Jasper. He'll make me feel self-conscious. "It's not necessary."

The look of doubt on the man's face is obvious. "I don't like the idea of you being down there by yourself with this man."

"I'll be all right. It's just—an old flame who's back in town," I admit.

Jasper's graying eyebrows shoot so high I swear they hit his hairline—and it's receding. "Miss—"

"It's okay," I say, interrupting him. I'm sure he knows who I'm referring to. He's known me forever. What other old flame could I possibly have? The man who ruined me supposedly forever in Paris.

Well, I'm not ruined anymore. I can stand on my own two feet and I've found a man who's much more caring and thoughtful than *he* could ever be.

"I'll be fine," I continue, even as he stares at me, his gaze full of doubt. I lift my chin, going for an abundance of confidence. Most likely failing miserably. "Truly it will take only a couple minutes of my time. Call security downstairs. Have them keep an eye on me while I'm there."

"I will," Jasper says firmly, sounding bossy as hell. "I'd prefer to accompany you downstairs. I'm sure Mr. Constantine would prefer it too."

Oh shit. Is he going to rat me out to Perry?

No. I can't have that. But this conversation needs to happen. I need to tell Seamus to back off once and for all. And though I might regret going down there and talking to him—God knows what he might say—I know this is the right thing for me to do. For myself.

And my marriage.

"Please don't mention this meeting to Perry, Jasper. I'll tell him everything tonight when he comes home." After we've had plenty of sex and he's relaxed and more open minded. "He'll just worry if you tell him about it now."

Jasper makes a harumphing noise. He is not pleased. "I don't like this idea."

"I'll be gone for ten minutes. Tops." I start to head for the door. "Call the security desk. Let him know I'm coming down. Then he can tell Seamus."

I glance down at myself, wondering if I should change. I'm in one of my favorite matching sweatsuits—all black, like my soul—that's what I used to tell Jasper, and he would always chuckle. I was fully planning on hopping in the shower before Seamus showed up and getting glammed up for my man for his dinner, which will be me. And some sort of takeout. That is still on the agenda.

And I definitely don't need to get glammed up for this man. God, I wish he would just leave me—us—alone.

"I'll be back in a few!" I call as I undo the locks and open the door. I head for the elevator, hitting the down button and waiting for only a minute tops before the doors slide open. I walk inside, turning to face them when I hear the apartment door swing open and the sound of Jasper's voice.

"Charlotte! You forgot your phone!"

The doors shut before I can stop them and I'm immediately filled with regret. The elevator is hurtling me down to the bottom floor and I contemplate hitting our floor's button again the moment it stops and coming right back up here. Seamus can wait a few extra minutes.

It would be safer if I had my phone on me.

But the moment the ding sounds and the doors slide open, I realize the lobby is bustling with activity and there's no need for me to have my phone. This interaction is going to be quick and hopefully painless.

Besides, there are so many witnesses.

I approach the security desk, about to ask one of the suited gentlemen where my visitor is when I hear his deep voice coming from directly behind me.

"Charlotte."

Slowly I turn to face him, and this time around, I really take him in. At the coffee shop on my wedding day, I'd been so shocked I really hadn't seen him. It was more like a haze had dropped over my eyes, making it difficult to see.

Or maybe I just didn't want to see him. Having Seamus in front of me after all that time without seeing him at all was too painful for me to deal with.

Now I study him, noting the extra silver at his temples. His inky-black hair and eyebrows and the matching dark scruff on his jaw. Turbulent brown eyes meet mine and I see regret there.

So much regret.

Well, too damn bad.

He was a handsome man then, and he still is. That hasn't changed. Only my feelings for him have.

I lift my chin, glaring at him. "Seamus."

His smile is small. Hopeful. "I'm so glad you agreed to meet with me. It's been—a while."

His familiar Irish brogue touched with a hint of Parisian makes my heart pang, but for only a second.

No. Not even a second. More like a blip, because the longer I look at him, hear his voice, see the way he's behaving, the angrier I get.

"I'm only talking to you because you're so damn persistent," I tell him, letting my anger fly. "I want you to leave me alone. I'm married. I have no interest in hearing what you have to say, or how much you regret how things ended between us. I don't care about any of it. Or you."

His gaze flickers with annoyance. "You really think I regret how things ended?"

Him picking up on that one particular sentence only makes me angrier. "I don't care if you do or don't regret it. I'm asking you politely to leave me alone. Do you understand?"

I'm about to turn and head back for the elevators when his cold words stop me.

"You know he's using you."

Glancing over my shoulder, I frown at him. "No more than you were using me."

"Suppose you're used to that sort of treatment, then. Such a pathetic little girl you are." His smile is not pleasant. It's dark and almost menacing. "The Constantines are utter trash."

I turn to face him fully once more. "Don't insult my family."

Seamus laughs but there's no humor in the sound. "They're not your *family*. I don't see them rallying around you and taking you into the Constantine fold. You're still holed up in this apartment, bought by Lancaster money. They have no plans on making you a true Constantine, Charlotte. You'll be running back to your parents' place within six months' time. I guarantee it."

I do my best not to flinch at his words, keeping myself in place. "That's not true."

"And how do you know that?"

I consider what I'm about to say and go for it. "Because my husband came inside me without a condom on just last night. And a few days ago, too. On our honeymoon. We want to have a baby."

That last part is a lie, but it sounds good. And it delivers just the reaction I'm looking for.

Seamus is furious.

"You're a fool," he mutters, taking a step forward. "Getting pregnant with his baby will ruin everything."

I glare at him. "We're *married.* We want to eventually start a family. That's the whole point."

He releases a shaky breath and I can practically feel the anger vibrating off of him, yet he doesn't say anything.

"This all feels really familiar," I say, thinking of the last time we ran into each other. He said basically the same thing to me then. "Leave me alone. If you try to contact me again, I'm going to file a restraining order."

I turn on my heel, about to march back toward the bank of elevators when he grabs hold of the crook of my elbow, something cold and steely jabbed against my rib cage. I suck in a sharp breath, glancing around the room, but no one is paying attention to us. Not even the men behind the security desk.

"Make one wrong move and I'll shoot you. I

don't care if I still crave the taste of your lips," he mutters close to my ear. "I will end you."

I give a jerky nod, keeping my head bent. The gun pressed against my side makes me feel faint. I need to cooperate. "What do you want from me?"

"I want you to leave with me without making a fuss." He presses the gun closer, and I whimper. "Now."

Slowly he turns us both so we're facing the double doors that lead outside. I walk beside him, trying to implore people as I walk past them with a look. A pained smile.

But they either smile in response and look away, or they don't make eye contact with me at all.

Once we're outside, the cold late October wind hits us and I shiver. He readjusts his hold on the gun, pressing it harder against my ribs and it's like my heart made its way into my throat. I can't swallow. I can barely breathe.

I told Jasper not to tell Perry, though I'm sure he will when I don't return quick enough. And I left my phone in the apartment. They can't even track me.

I fell right into this man's hands, and he didn't have to do a damn thing but show up.

"Get in the car," Seamus orders, shoving me

toward the sleek black sports car that sits by the curb. I open the door, glancing over my shoulder at him, and he's so close, I'm almost afraid he's going to do something crazy like…

Kiss me.

"Get in," he growls, his gaze on my mouth.

Like a scared little mouse, I leap into the passenger seat, jumping when he slams the door. He rounds the front of the car quickly, not giving me enough time to escape, and then he's starting the engine and we're pulling away, much like Perry and I did only last night.

"Where are you taking me?" I ask, my voice quiet. Eerily calm.

"You'll see," he says, his gaze on the road. "Hand over your phone."

"I didn't bring it with me."

He jerks his head in my direction, his gaze sharp. "I don't believe you. Hand it over."

"I left it in my apartment, I swear."

He comes to a stop at a red light, and the next thing I know, his hands are all over me, patting me down, searching for my phone. I try to fend him off, batting at his hands, trying to make a scene in case I catch the attention of the people in the stopped cars around us.

Seamus slaps my face quick as lightning, effectively stopping me. I cry out, resting my palm against my cheek as I stare at him in horror.

"Keep it up and I'll do worse than that to you," he warns, his voice stern.

"Who are you?" I whisper shakily, shock coursing through my veins, leaving me ice cold.

His smile is pure evil. "The man you should've married."

CHAPTER TWENTY-FOUR

Perry

A LAST-MINUTE MEETING is scheduled at three thirty and I send Charlotte a quick text, letting her know I'll be a little late for my "dinner."

No response.

I sit in the meeting that lasts longer than an hour, bored out of my skull and unable to check my phone thanks to my grumpy-ass brother who glares at me every time I so much as reach for it in my pocket. It's like if he has to suffer, I do too and so I sit there and listen to the chief financial officer drone on about budgets and bullshit. Eventually my mind drifts and I daydream about my wife.

Can't get over the moment in the parking garage last night. Or when I fingered her right before we went into the diner. But it was more than that. It was—fun, sitting with her in the diner and eating milkshakes and burgers with her. Teasing her, the entire moment lighthearted. Until it got hot and heavy.

I liked both aspects of the evening. Sex with my wife is getting better and better. We're understanding each other. Enjoying each other's bodies. Learning what the other likes.

I'm not used to this sort of thing. Back in the day, I'd have sex with one woman, maybe a couple of times, normally only once, and then move on to the next one.

No way would I ever admit it to anyone, but I'm digging this monogamy stuff.

The moment the meeting is finished, I'm leaping from my chair, ready to hustle my ass out of there and get to my wife when Winston stops me.

"Talk to me a minute," he demands, striding toward his office.

Pissed, I follow him in there, slamming the door shut behind me. "What?"

He turns, narrowing his eyes. "What's got you all twisted up?"

"I need to get home."

Winston grins. "Wifey waiting for you on the dining room table naked?"

Now there's an image.

"I hope to fuck so," I mutter.

"I'll make this quick, then. Myron is looking into the texts. Said they're from a burner phone. One of those prepaid things you get at a drugstore or whatever."

"Could've already told you that."

"Yeah, well, it's a specific brand that's only sold at a specific chain store."

"Which one?"

When he gives me the name, I make a dismissive noise. "We'll never figure out who purchased it."

"Myron could. He's a miracle worker. Let's give him a chance."

I shove my hands in my pockets, my fingers curling around my phone. "Is that all you wanted to tell me?"

Winston nods. "I'll let you know what he finds out."

"Cool. Hey, I appreciate you helping me with this." I feel like a jackass for acting shitty.

"Of course."

I pull my phone out of my pocket to see I have a text from…

An unknown number.

"What the fuck?" I mutter as I open my

phone with face recognition and go into my text messages. What I see makes my heart drop into my fucking balls.

Makes me want to rip someone's fucking heart out.

It's a photo of Charlotte, her hands and feet bound with rope, a piece of duct tape around her mouth. Her eyes are wide and pleading and she's got on her favorite black matching sweatsuit. She told me when she wears it, she feels like she's Doja's mother, since the cat is all black too.

My wife is weird. Adorable. Sexy.

And currently being held captive by this motherfucker who sent me the image along with a threatening text.

> ***Unknown number:*** *I've got what I've always wanted. Want it back? Wait for my next message. And whatever you do, don't get the police involved.*

"He's got her." I thrust the phone in Winston's face, panic zipping through my veins. "That motherfucker *stole* her from me."

Winston blinks at the image I show him, his gaze slowly lifting to mine. "Shit," he spits out. "That McTiernan asshole? Is he working for the Morellis?"

"Of course." I start texting, my fingers shaking with a mixture of fear and fury.

> **Me:** *You better not touch a single hair on her head or there will be hell to pay, you fucking asshole.*

"We should call the police," Winston suggests.

I shake my head. "He said not to involve the authorities."

"And what's he going to do? He won't hurt her. She's the most valuable thing he's got," Winston says.

That's the problem. She's the most valuable thing in the world. My world. The Chevelle isn't my most prized possession.

My wife is.

Another photo comes through, this one with a gun pointed at Charlotte's forehead, her eyes squeezed tightly shut, tears streaking down her cheeks.

"Oh God." The agonized sound is ripped from my chest and I scrub a hand over my face, waiting for more.

He doesn't disappoint.

> **Unknown number:** *I'm watching you. You call the cops, I'll end her. I promise. Don't fuck with me. Wait for my instructions.*

Me: *Tell me what you want.*

Unknown number: *Not now. Later.*

Me: *When?*

Unknown number: *When I'm ready.*

I lift my head to stare at my brother. "We have to find her."

Winston goes to his desk and picks up the phone, hitting a number on speed dial. "On it."

"And when I find who took her." I pause for only a second, my world spinning completely out of control. "I'm going to kill him."

✧ ✧ ✧

Thank you for reading THE RUTHLESS GROOM by Monica Murphy!

We hope you love this sexy modern take on an arranged marriage... and we have more angst, drama, and scorching hot scenes to come. Find out what happens next for Charlotte Lancaster in THE RECKLESS UNION...

Our marriage may look like a fairytale, but outside forces threaten to tear us apart. Don't they realize that nothing will keep me apart from Charlotte? Not my family. Not hers either.

What started out as a relationship in name only has evolved into something much more. Something deeper. And when Charlotte is taken from me, I launch into action, determined to rescue her.

She's mine. Nothing is going to stop me from being with her.

Not a damn thing.

And you can read Winston Constantine's story right now!

Money can buy anything. And anyone. As the head of the Constantine family, I'm used to people bowing to my will. Cruel, rigid, unyielding—I'm all those things. When I discover the one woman who doesn't wither under my gaze, but instead smiles right back at me, I'm intrigued.

> "K. Webster has created a tale that's unapologetically, deliciously decadent. Extravagant sex, shocking fantasy, and wonderful humor too. I fell into it like a dream…a dream I didn't want to wake up from."
>
> – Annabel Joseph, New York Times bestselling author

The warring Morelli and Constantine families have enough bad blood to fill an ocean, and their brand new stories will be told by your favorite dangerous romance authors. See what books are available now and sign up to get notified about new releases here…
www.dangerouspress.com

ABOUT MIDNIGHT DYNASTY

The warring Morelli and Constantine families have enough bad blood to fill an ocean, and their brand new stories will be told by your favorite dangerous romance authors.

The new girl doesn't belong here.
So why can't I stop thinking about her?

I'm Keaton Constantine. My duty is to my family. At least, it was until I started unbraiding the good girl and realizing there's more to life than duty.

"A forbidden romance full of angst and delicious desire. Wicked Idol is unputdownable and so scorching hot it will melt your kindle. You're not going to want to leave Pembroke Prep."

– Amazon Top #10 bestselling author
Ivy Smoak

And Caroline Constantine has a resident fixer…

Outside a glittering party, I saw a man in the dark. I didn't know then that he was an assassin. A hit man. A mercenary. Ronan radiated danger and beauty. Mercy and mystery.

"This book grabbed me by the throat and dragged me into a dark alley…and I loved every minute of it!"

– USA Today bestselling author Katee Robert

As Father Magnus Falke, I suppress my cravings. As the headteacher of a Catholic boarding school, I'm never tempted by a student. Until her…

I became a priest to control my impulses.

Then I meet Tinsley Constantine.

> "Pam Godwin has penned a sinfully beautiful masterpiece in Lessons in Sin. An absolute must-read for lovers of dark and dangerous romance!"
>
> – Trisha Wolfe, author of Born, Darkly

SIGN UP FOR THE NEWSLETTER
www.dangerouspress.com

JOIN THE FACEBOOK GROUP HERE
www.dangerouspress.com/facebook

FOLLOW US ON INSTAGRAM
www.instagram.com/dangerouspress

ABOUT THE AUTHOR

Monica Murphy is the New York Times and USA Today bestselling author of the One Week Girlfriend series, the Billionaire Bachelors and The Rules series. Her books have been translated in almost a dozen languages and has sold over one million copies worldwide. She is both a traditionally published author and an independently published author. She writes new adult, young adult and contemporary romance. She is also USA Today bestselling romance author Karen Erickson.

She is a wife and a mother of three who lives with her family in central California on fourteen acres in the middle of nowhere, along with their one dog and too many cats. A self-confessed workaholic, when she's not writing, she's reading or hanging out with her husband and kids. She's a firm believer in happy endings, though she will admit to putting her characters through many angst-filled moments before they finally get that hard won HEA.

Learn more at monicamurphyauthor.com.

NEWSLETTER:
https://bit.ly/3tonW57

FACEBOOK READER GROUP:
https://bit.ly/34VoZA1

INSTAGRAM:
https://bit.ly/3MZYHOt

Copyright

Print Edition

Cover design: Damonza

Made in the USA
Monee, IL
02 August 2022

10779555R00176